"Having started out at a high level of ingenuity and humor, Barnard gets better, novel by novel."
—*The Washington Post*

High Praise of Four-Time Edgar Nominee
Robert Barnard

"One of the most winning talents to emerge on the crime scene." —*The Washington Post*

"You can count on a Barnard mystery being witty, intelligent, and a joy to read."
—*Publishers Weekly*

"Another of the author's unfailingly entertaining forays into crime." —*Kirkus Reviews*

"One of England's most skillful and sardonic writers." —*St. Louis Post-Dispatch*

"Barnard is an amusing Englishman with an eye for the self-delusion and hypocrisy in all of us . . . and the result is a growing series of mysteries that are entertaining, often quite funny . . . and acutely observing." —*The Boston Globe*

BY THE SAME AUTHOR:

The Cherry Blossom Corpse
Political Suicide
Fête Fatale
Out of the Blackout
Corpse in a Gilded Cage
School for Murder
The Case of the Missing Brontë
A Little Local Murder
Death and the Princess
Death by Sheer Torture
Death in a Cold Climate
Death of a Perfect Mother
Death of a Literary Widow
Death of a Mystery Writer

Bodies

Robert Barnard

A DELL BOOK

Published by
Dell Publishing
a division of
The Bantam Doubleday Dell Publishing Group, Inc.
1 Dag Hammarskjold Plaza
New York, New York 10017

Dell ® TM 681510, Dell Publishing, a division of the Bantam Doubleday Dell Publishing Group, Inc.

ISBN: 0-440-20007-5

Reprinted by arrangement with Charles Scribner's Sons

Printed in the United States of America

May 1988

10 9 8 7 6 5 4 3 2 1

KRI

For Louise, again

Bodies

CHAPTER 1

Take a casual glance at Phil Fennilow and you would put him down as the typical, grubby-raincoated purchaser of pornography. I often used to see him, some years ago, when I was part of an investigation into corruption in the Metropolitan Police Vice Squad—an investigation which resembled trying to root out maggots from Gorgonzola cheese. Regularly at about half past nine in the morning he would emerge from the Leicester Square underground station, drawing around him that grubby mac which he wore in all weathers, and scuttle along the main streets on the fringes of Soho until he turned into a miserable doorway and scurried

up the stairs. The plate on the doorway read HEALTH
AND VITALITY PUBLICATIONS, and though I once or
twice lingered around, I never saw him emerge carrying books or magazines in a brown paper wrapping, as
the archetypal grubby-raincoated figure ought to have
done. It was a long time before I twigged that Phil
Fennilow did not purchase porn, he published it—or
rather, he edited a monthly periodical which, to the
censorious, might have come under the heading of soft
porn, though even they would have had to admit that it
came at the fairly harmless, more enjoyable end of the
soft porn spectrum—so soft, in fact, as to be practically
marshmallow. The title of the magazine was *Bodies*.

I saw him often, as I say, during that investigation,
and even talked to him once, in a pub at lunch-time. But
my real professional interest in him began on a bitter
November morning in 198-. On that day Phil did not
alter his routine (he told me all this that same day,
during our first interview, and I never had reason to
doubt that, as far as it went, he spoke the truth). He
came up the escalator from the Northern Line, clutching his *Daily Telegraph,* and emerged as usual, blinking
behind his thick spectacles, into the drizzle, pulling his
raincoat around him. It was not the raincoat I had been
used to see him wearing, but it too had got dirty, or else
it had never been clean. He dived off the square into
the shabby streets, and he made like a homing pigeon
for his office. Phil, I later discovered, knew almost nothing of the rest of London, beyond his chosen route, and
he would mention Whitehall as if it were foreign terri-
tory. When he got inside the doorway he shook the rain
from his coat, mounted the dingy staircase in his
sprightly crab-like manner, shouted " 'Morning, Bob"

as he walked past the brightly lit studio, then went into his office. He took off his raincoat, and settled down to work.

The morning's correspondence was along standard lines: letters asking for the addresses of people (bodies, perhaps I should say) whose picture had appeared in the magazine; letters from health cranks, from anti-porn campaigners, from semi-literate teenagers, most of the last wanting to "brake into moddling," as one of them put it. There was a letter from a clergyman who offered to put up a thousand pounds towards a film of *Lesbia Brandon.* To him Phil replied that very much more would be necessary to produce a film of any quality; to the seekers of addresses he sent a firm no; for the rest he had standard form replies. The mail answered, he started in on the proof-reading for the December *Bodies.*

The text of the magazine was not its most important feature, and he had, in fact, very nearly finished the task when something that had been nagging away at the back of his mind pushed its way unanswerably to the front: why was it so quiet? There was traffic noise outside, of course, and the usual sounds from the brothel next door as they coped with the early influx of night-shift workers. But where were the noises from inside the premises of Health and Vitality Publications? Bob Cordle was a quiet, efficient workman, but inevitably there were sounds: directions to the models, a flash exploding, equipment being moved. Then another thought struck him, and he looked for confirmation at the masthead of his *Telegraph:* it was Thursday. Bob never worked in the *Bodies* studio on Thursday mornings, or almost never. It was the day he photographed half-timbered houses for the *Essex Countryside*. He often worked on Wednesday evenings, but not on Thursday mornings.

But if he wasn't working today, why had the lights been on? Bob was always very careful, and he knew that economy with any electrical appliance was one of Phil's little foibles.

Phil Fennilow sat back in his chair and listened. Nothing. He got up, hesitantly, and went to the door. Still there was light blazing from the crack in the studio door, but no sound. Phil was not embarrassed about breaking in on one of Bob's sessions: the poses were always perfectly decent, and there was never any hanky-panky going on because that wouldn't have been *Bodies* style at all. Practically a family magazine, as Phil always said. But what Phil felt was that Bob was an artist, and he shouldn't be interrupted—"any more," as he afterwards expressed it to me, "than I'd've barged in on Whistler when 'e was painting 'is muvver-in-law." So he stood there for a full minute before, finding the silence eerie, he walked down the passage and quietly pushed open the door.

"OH! Oh my Gawd! Help!"

With rising panic he began to run, stumbling down the stairs, screaming and calling for help. He arrived at the bottom almost in a heap, ran along the passage, and then out of the doorway into Windlesham Street. "Help! Oh my Gawd, help!" he was crying still. To his enormous relief he practically ran into the arms of a police constable (for this was, after all, Soho).

When I got there, about an hour later, they had let Phil go and lie down on the sofa in the little room off from his office. He was still in a state of near-hysteria, and they feared that his heart would give way.

"It was all those bodies," he kept babbling apologetically. "I can't get over the sight of all those bodies."

CHAPTER 2

It was eleven o'clock before I got the detail for the Health and Vitality murders. "You're just the man," said Joe Grierley, my superior. "There's a lot of you, and there's a lot of them." My name is Perry Trethowan, by the way, and I tend to get landed with cases that have snob associations or literary ones. I think Joe—God help him—classed this one among the literary ones.

I was in Windlesham Street by eleven-fifteen, and (perhaps to demonstrate my health and vitality) I bounded up the stairs to the first floor. It was spurious activity, because my time had not come yet. The technicians were in their first frenzy of busy-ness, and beyond registering first impressions there was not a great deal I could do. I stood in the doorway, and for the first time really took in the scale of the investigation I was embarking on. By the scale of massacres—St. Bartholomew's, say, or St. Valentine's—this one was very small: only four. I wondered who in the Calendar of Saints had presided over this little affair.

The unnaturally bright light in the room certainly enabled me to get a good view of the set-up. Glaring spots were positioned on both sides of the studio, focused on the far wall. A couple of feet from the door cameras were set up, and it was by them that the two bodies were sprawled. One was a squat, pot-bellied man in his shirtsleeves, the other a lanky boy of, I guessed, no more than twenty.

The lights beat hardest on the other two. They had clearly been killed last. The woman had backed as if in terror, and put her arms over her body, as if they could be some protection. The man seemed to have been starting forward. She had light brown hair, was full-breasted with creamy skin. He, face down, was six feet tall, with a well-muscled back and strong thighs. Considered as bodies, they were perfect.

There was nothing more to be done there for a bit. A sergeant directed me to Phil Fennilow's office, and told me that the editor himself was lying down on a bed in the little office next door to his own. I nodded, and went very quietly along to Phil's sanctum. It suited me to have a look round without his presence. Something, it was quite clear, had been going on in the offices of *Bodies*, and I wanted to know if it was with or without the knowledge of the editor.

The office was seedy in the extreme, and probably

dirty to boot. In the studio, lights and drapes had hidden the seediness, but here it was thrust at one. Not somewhere, I thought, that Phil would bring anyone he wanted to impress, if any such person existed. There was a desk, a desk chair, and an armchair with springs that poked out like ostentatious muscle. One small table with *Bodies* piled up on it, and a few rickety bookshelves, piled with magazines and books. The calendars on the walls displayed, all too predictably, bodies.

I first flipped through the correspondence on the desk. I've mentioned some of the letters already, and there were others spiked. Most of them were from readers, regular models, or subscribers annoyed about the magazine's non-arrival. There was a little pile of shrieks to the paper's agony aunt. All was fairly predictable, including those complaints about the non-arrival of the magazine: the police, I had no doubt, would on occasion check *Bodies* to see whether it had changed its character and become openly pornographic. No doubt the missing copies were now, in a well-thumbed condition, adorning police canteens somewhere or other in London.

I decided it wouldn't be a bad idea if I made a similar check on the current state of the magazine. The last five or six issues were stacked on the small table by the door, and I took them over to the armchair, which fought back as I sat down on it. Then I flipped through the most recent *Bodies*.

I had to hand it to Phil Fennilow: *Bodies* was a damned good idea. It consisted almost entirely of pictures of people with nice bodies. Nice bodies, be it said, of all kinds: there were busty ladies and boyish girls, there were musclemen and girlish boys. It was a magazine, therefore, that did not stamp the sexual orientation of the buyer. It could be bought without embarrassment by a homosexual in Barnsley or a heterosexual in Bayswater. There was one other clever point about it. Large parts of the magazine were made up of pictures sent in by readers. They did use models as well, of course, as the bodies in the studio made only too clear: there were professionals posing in briefs or tastefully naked (genitals were avoided, or merely "suggested"), sometimes in color, usually smiling and bursting with health. These models, no doubt, had to be paid, though probably much less than if there had been anything erotic or explicit about the poses. But at least two double pages of each issue would be taken up with a spread of readers' pictures—of themselves, their loved ones, their children—and every month there was a "star" picture, that had one page to itself, and earned the lucky reader the princely sum of £10. It was wonderfully cheap, and good for reader-relations as well. Was Phil proprietor as well as editor of the magazine, I wondered? If so, he was probably coining it in.

There were other features each month, to fill up the space. There was a sort of editorial, full of avuncular heartiness to the "boys and girls" who read the paper. There was an interview with a "personality," who told readers how he or she took care of their body. There was an advice column, answering readers' questions—medical questions, queries about diet or exercise routines, occasional sexual problems, delicately framed. There was a column about exercises that dealt with a different part of the body each month ("Don't Neglect Your Diaphragm"). One did not need the sort of exhaustive computer tests that supposedly have proved Shake-

speare to be the author of *Sir Thomas More* to conclude
that each and every one of these regular features was
written by Phil Fennilow. Coining it in, as I said.

The important thing that I registered, though, was
that *Bodies* was pretty much the same today as when I
had last seen it, ten or twelve years before. Why alter a
winning formula? It was not now, anymore than it had
been then, an indecent publication. Unless there was a
dark undercurrent somewhere along the line that I was
too naive to have detected, it seemed to be by and large
a perfectly healthy product.

Which was more than you could say for Phil Fennilow. He must finally have heard me moving about in
his office, because suddenly the door into the side room
opened, and there he was.

"Oh my Gawd, I feel rotten," he wheezed. "Where's
me fags?"

It didn't seem the time, though it was certainly the
place, to preach the virtues of non-smoking. I pointed to
a packet of a tipless brand on his desk.

"You look as if you could do with a drink," I said. "Got
any?"

"There's some brandy somewhere," said Phil. "Try
one of the lower drawers."

I found it, a very dusty bottle. That wasn't one of
Phil's vices, then. I poured him a drink in a rather
greasy glass, not wanting to disturb any evidence there
might be in the washroom. Phil didn't notice the dirt.
He drank it down in a succession of increasingly large
sips. As he did so, I watched him. He wasn't, it must be
said, a very prepossessing sight. His fingers were deeply
stained with nicotine, his shirt hung limply on a hollow-
chested body, and his cheeks were hollow too, with an

unhealthy yellow tinge to them. His teeth looked as if they had not been bared to a dentist in decades, and his eyes were dull behind his thick spectacles. All in all, as an advertisement for the advice he peddled, he was a dead loss. But perhaps, like so many great editors, he represented his typical reader.

"Oh my Gawd," he said again, and was immediately doubled up by a hacking cough. "It's the shock."

"You found them, I believe?"

" 'Course I bleeding found them. 'Orrible. Gave me the screaming ab-dabs." *gawd ones!*

"Could you tell me about it?"

"S'pose I got to, some time or other."

So, sitting down at his desk, and dragging deeply on his cigarette, he did tell me—pretty much as I've told it to you already, though I've added the odd aspirate here and there. When he got to the point where he opened the studio door, I asked:

"You saw—what?"

"All them bleeding bodies, o' course."

"You recognized them?"

"I didn't stop to recognize them. I just ran."

"Who do you think they were?"

He considered for a moment, and actually shuddered.

"Well, I assumed it was Bob by the camera nearest to the door. Bob Cordle."

"What is Bob like?"

"Nice bloke. Lovely bloke—"

*"Phys*ically."

"Oh—well, fairly short, got a bit of a pot on him . . . starting to bald . . ."

"Sounds like Bob Cordle," I said, making a note. "Know any of the others?"

"There was another by the cameras, wasn't there?"

"That's right."

"That could be Dale 'Erbert. Young lad. Bob used to let him string along, partly as helper, partly to learn the trade. He was a sort of unemployed student, see."

"Lanky lad, about twenty?"

"That's it . . . Poor little bugger. 'E didn't 'ave much of a life, did 'e?"

"What about the others? The models?"

"Didn't see, mate. Wasn't close enough. 'E was face dahn, anyway, so I couldn't see. And she was sort of turned away. I didn't go into the room, see. Well, who bleeding well would? Like a bloody morgue, it was."

My experience of morgues was that they were at least well-conducted places. Still, I could well imagine that any civilian, faced with the sight of Phil's studio, would have obeyed that first instinct to run.

"So you've no idea who he was planning to use as models last night?"

"No, mate. Could have been anyone. 'Course, he had his favourite regular models—so it could have been Cindy, or Melissa, or Mary Jane . . . And the bloke might have been Ted, or Clive . . ."

"Did he keep a notebook of names?" I interrupted.

"Yes. Always had it with him. Then if one let him dahn, 'e'd get on the blower to someone else. You'll probably find it on him now."

"Right, I'll look. Tell me about that studio through there. Is it just used for taking the photographs for *Bodies*?"

"Oh no. We're only a monthly, and we like to take a

lot of our shots outdoors, if we can. More 'ealthy, like. So there was plenty of free capacity, as you might say. The arrangement was basically that I leased it out to Bob. He used it for his own work mainly on Monday and Wednesday mornings, and Friday afternoons. Other times—like Wednesday afternoons—he used it for our work. He paid me rent, of course—gentleman's agreement."

"What exactly was his own work?"

"What are you lookin' so suspicious for?" I didn't know I had been. Phil was sharp. "It wasn't anything sordid, I can tell you that, and if you'd've known Bob you'd never 'ave got the idea. No, a lot of the people he meets in this business need publicity shots. Quite a few of the girls are dancers, actresses, that sort of thing. They need stacks of photos for agents and producers— different poses, different moods, you know how it is. And some of the men do stage work as well, and some are professional bodybuilders. So there was always a call for other sorts of photographic material—the sort of thing we wouldn't be interested in. Particularly as he was very tasteful, was Bob. Perfect gent in every way."

"The Sir Galahad of the zoom lens," I said, not bothering to conceal my skepticism.

"Sarky, aren't you? Well, he was, and all 'is pals will say the same."

"And were his models always similarly perfect ladies and gents?"

"No-o-o. No, you couldn't say that—in the nature of things that wouldn't be likely, would it? Some of the girls was on the game, at least part-time. We wouldn't use anyone *tarty*, that wouldn't be right for the image, but if they was good models we couldn't be too sniffy about their other activities."

"And the men?"

"Well, some of *them* was on the game too, to be frank. Or there'd be the odd nightclub bouncer, sportsman, bodyguard, that kind of thing. The sort of person who's making a living doing a bit of this and a bit of that."

"Ye-e-es. Sometimes on the borders between the legal and the criminal, I suppose."

"That's your business, ain't it? It wasn't our duty to run along and inform on them."

"No, no—I'm just trying to get the picture. Now, what do you think happened yesterday?"

"Christ, mate, I shudder to think. I'm trying to shove it out of my mind. Thank God that's for you to find out."

"What I meant was, he was doing work for you in the evening, was he?"

"That's right. Wednesday afternoons and early evenings (for the convenience of models with nine to five jobs) he was always doing stuff for *Bodies*. Thursday mornings he was never in, which is what made me suspicious in the first place."

"The bodies look as if they have been dead some hours. Say, provisionally, they were killed some time during that session. How long were you here into the session?"

Phil Fennilow coughed, and then put another fag in.

"Till abaht quarter to five."

"Did you see him?"

" 'Eard 'im," he said. " 'Eard 'im arrive about half three, or maybe closer to four."

"You were here in this office?"

"That's right. I was doing the advice column."

"That's mostly medical advice, isn't it?"

"Partly." He became all defensive. "I've got this doctor pal I ring up. Anyway, I've done it so long now I know most of the answers. I'm a sort of common law doctor."

"I see. And you heard Bob Cordle arrive. Did you speak to each other?"

"He shouted ' 'Afternoon, Phil,' same as usual, and I shouted back. We'd always have a good old confab when he was going through the shots for the next issue, and now and again we'd go to the Green Man and have a drink, but otherwise, he'd go 'is way, and I'd go mine."

"Did you hear other people arrive?"

"Yes . . . yes, I think so. But that was normal, see— routine. I didn't take particular notice. There was other people there when I left."

"Ah—you heard them?"

"Yes. Well, I heard *him* talking to them."

"What was he saying?"

Phil considered again.

"Something like: 'Put your chin up, darling, then your bos'll show up better.' Again, routine, like I say."

"A woman, then. No indication of a man being there?"

"No, but he could easily have been there already. Or of course Bob could have had several sessions lined up. The chap could have come along later, or Bob could have had a solo session with the girl, then an entirely different couple come along later."

"In which case I'd definitely like to find the girl . . ."

"Sometimes the sessions only lasted an hour. They were pretty experienced models, some of them."

"But I suppose you and he were always on the lookout for new bodies?"

"Oh yes. Then it would take longer. Some of them would just stand there grinning like they was in a 'oliday camp snapshot. 'E was very good with that kind . . . patient."

"And of course a *touch* of amateurism doesn't go amiss with *Bodies*, does it? It's part of the appeal."

"Well, yes, in a way. We aim to give the feeling of one big 'appy family. Like it's a sort of game that everybody can join in. See, lots of blokes like fat girls, so we always 'ave a fat girl somewhere in the issue. Makes 'em feel wanted. The idea is that all bodies are attractive in their way."

I was politely refraining from looking skeptically at his own body when Phil, who had been recovering somewhat, suddenly looked at me hard.

" 'Ere," he said, " 'aven't I seen you before? 'Ad a confab with you somewhere?"

"That's right," I said, getting up. "Well, they must be finishing in there. I think I'll go and have a look."

CHAPTER 3

When I got back to the door of the studio, near to the head of the stairs, it was clear that the first burst of energy in this particular investigation was coming to an end. The crowd of police was thinning out, and the atmosphere was far less hectic. Soon the scientists would have done their job, and I could begin the investigation proper: data being on record, one could get to the heart of the matter, people. I looked at those four bodies, still in place: the chalk marks around them, and the tape measures left on the floor, somehow made their deaths unreal, reduced their humanity. They looked like models posing for a forensic science lecture.

I stood at the door and had a word with the newly created Inspector Joplin, one of the youngest in the force, and a bright, sharp, noticing type. I had left him in charge of the studio, to collate all the early information.

"Anything solid?" I asked.

"Some very solid bodies," he replied, nodding his head inwards to the corpses. "But before you have a look at them, will you come and cast your eye at the stairs?" He led me to the top of them, and we looked down towards the door, open on to Windlesham Street. "Now, first, the technical people think the place was cleaned yesterday."

"They should take a look at Phil Fennilow's office," I said.

"Ah, but that's a bit different, isn't it? There's lots of people don't like their offices being touched, and I can imagine that Mr. Fennilow is the sort that has his own messy methods. But the studio is in a way the door to the outside world, isn't it? The models see it, and the readers see it in the photographs. It seems to have been kept pretty clean, on an obvious level—floors washed, window-ledges and mantelpiece wiped over—that sort of thing. There's just a very light coating of dust, such as you always get in these old buildings."

"Right. And I take it the same is true of the stairs?"

"We think so, though there's rather more dust on them, from the street. The door's open much of the day, apparently. Now—most of these footprints are a bit of a jumble—they've been done today by our men, of course, a lot of them. It's easy enough to eliminate us, and Fennilow, and the four stiffs upstairs . . . and that leaves three or four prints unaccounted for. Nothing surprising in that, and you'll get details of all of them, naturally. But the prints that rather interested me were *those.*"

He pointed to an impression in the dust six steps down, where it was coming away from the jumble of prints in the middle of the stairs. It was a solid, well-defined print.

"Rather as if he stopped," I said.

"That's what I thought. Stopped and listened, perhaps."

"And he was going from the centre, towards the staircase wall, to see if he could see in through the studio door."

"Right," said Joplin. "Which at that point, depending on his height, he probably could do. Then he starts again—see there's another right-hand shoe on the fourth down, a left one on the third. He's keeping to the wall, you notice."

"But these are a bit lighter, aren't they? Faster?"

"They are, and so are those across the little passageway until . . . *here.* We're willing to bet that's the same shoe."

He pointed to a smudged and partial impression in the doorway of the studio.

"And inside?"

"Nothing. If that was our man—or woman—they just shot them up, and left. There are one or two marks that we think are him charging downstairs."

"Him or her. As you say, it could be a woman. It's a fairly small shoe, isn't it? It looks to me as if it could be some kind of jogging shoe."

"That's what the experts thought. In which case the

male and female versions are pretty much alike. The
size, we thought, was about six or six and a half."

"Interesting. You'd expect one of those muscle boys
to have bigger feet than that."

"Not necessarily. Often they're not particularly tall,
or naturally big. Glamour boy in there only takes seven
and a halfs."

"Inside every muscle man there is a six-stone weakling crying to come out," I pontificated. "And he shows
through the feet. Right, I presume there'll be casts of all
the interesting prints? Let's go into the studio."

Now that there were fewer CID men around, and
now that I could move around without holding my
breath, I could get a better idea of Health and Vitality's
studio. It was a good-sized room, perhaps thirteen feet
or so by twenty-five, and though it was decorated in a
nondescript white, colour was added by the blue satin
drape that was hung over the far wall. In a pile near the
fireplace were ten or twelve other coloured materials,
no doubt alternative drapes. The fireplace itself, an
early nineteenth-century job if my eye didn't deceive
me, had been picked out in blue and white in a mock-
Wedgwood sort of way, and no doubt it served as a
"feature" for occasional poses. The floor was a nondescript lino, but again there were various rugs around,
clean and spruce, that no doubt could be used for certain types of shots. There was a large window overlook-
ing Windlesham Street, but it had a white drape pinned
over it. Of furniture there was none, though I had registered a door outside that could possibly lead to a store-
room. Surely for some of the shots they might use a sofa,
or chairs? The bareness of the room had meant that the
models' clothes had been left in piles on the floor. The

man had had a holdall, and had left a tracksuit carefully folded on top of it. The girl had left her clothes piled neatly on top of an *Evening Standard*. Both had registered, presumably, the slight film of dust on everything.

"Now, how did they die?" I asked.

"Bullets from a thirty-two automatic," said Joplin, reeling it off from his notebook. "This boy here—"

He pointed to the lanky body behind the cameras.

"I think his name might be Herbert," I said.

"It is. Dale Herbert. We've found his student card. He was shot twice. Apparently the first only got him in the shoulder. The girl was also shot twice, though Doc thinks the first in fact killed her. Just finishing off the round, I suppose."

"A man who knew how to handle a gun, then."

"Certainly no novice. A man with real training, even if not necessarily a hired killer. You'll get a report on the bullets eventually, but ballistics suspects a rather elderly automatic. One of the bullets went through the girl, and we picked it up off the floor, so they've had a good look at it."

"Right. Now, who are they?"

"The only one we're not sure of is the man. The model, I mean. There's no name on the holdall, and the only clothes are the tracksuit, running shoes, boxer shorts and so on. We reckon he'd been at a track, or a gym. Oh, there is a birthday card in the holdall, with 'Love from Debbie' on it."

"Some birthday present *he's* had," I commented. "What about the others? The cameraman I take it is Bob Cordle?"

"That's it. All the cameras and their boxes are labelled, and there's a bank card in his wallet. Dale Herbert seems to have been a student at the City of London Poly, by the way, so there shouldn't be any trouble tracing him. The girl's a student too, funnily enough."

"Really?"

"That's right. Probably post-grad, I'd say, because she's twenty-four. Name of Susan Platt-Morrison. Apparently a student at Bedford College. There's also a letter in her handbag from 'Mummy'—headed notepaper, address in the Thames Valley."

"I see. Do you think Mummy in the Thames Valley knew she modelled for *Bodies?* No doubt we'll find that out before long. Well, we seem to be getting there. I suppose I'd better have my own look at the bodies before they're carted off."

It wasn't something I ever liked doing. (Many policemen do, by the way—some in a completely abstract way which springs from the fact that murder cases are for us what high C's are for a tenor, others in a way that leaves no one in any doubt of the frank enjoyment they extract from the contemplation of violence and death.) Four bodies simultaneously was something new in my experience, apart from my one IRA bomb. These four had all died very quickly, that was clear, but three of them at least had had a second or two of terrified anticipation. Bob Cordle, I guessed, had been crouched behind his camera and had known nothing until the bullet entered his back. Dale Herbert seemed to have turned in the direction of the door, and was presumably shot second. He was—he had been—a long, scruffy, amiable-looking youth. Bob Cordle was shortish, balding and pot-bellied, wearing a cardigan and old-fashioned grey flannels.

"There was a notebook in his jacket pocket," said

Joplin. "It looked interesting. The boys will let you have it as soon as they've done with it."

"Good," I said. "We may need it to identify the man, if Phil Fennilow doesn't know him."

The models, it had to be presumed, had had longer to anticipate death: not long in real terms, but long enough to them. The girl was full-figured, light brown-haired, with what one guessed had been a very attractive face. It was heavily made up, as probably it had to be, even for that apostle of the natural, *Bodies* magazine. But the make-up was done skilfully, and there was no suggestion of the tart. I turned over the clothes, which, similarly, were smart and good, not smart and tart. I guessed at a girl who liked the good things of life, but was not extracting enough money out of the Thames Valley to buy them. The man was more difficult. Men always are, but particularly so in this case. Shorts and tracksuit and jogging shoes don't tell you much, and you could guess he was some kind of athlete from the body alone. The bag held the card Joplin had mentioned, a bodybuilding magazine, and a jock strap. The body itself told one little, except that he had dedicated himself to making it beautiful.

"Mr. Anonymous," I said. "Nothing but a collection of pectorals and biceps brachis."

"You're not without pectorals and biceps brachis yourself," said Joplin.

"Sorry. Was I moralizing? I mustn't get into the *Hamlet* syndrome every time I see a corpse. No doubt eventually the young man will acquire a name and a personality. Well then—four bodies and six shots, and nobody reported anything to the police at the time. Isn't it wonderful? Still, I suppose you could say that was Soho."

"Soho isn't all crooks," protested Joplin. "After all, it's fifty percent restaurants."

"Whose proprietors take very good care not to get on the wrong side of the crooks," I said. "They'll keep very quiet until we go asking—then they'll have to weigh up which side in the crime war they prefer to keep on the right side of."

I drew back the drape from the window and looked along the street.

"Chinese opposite. Greek three doors down. I used to go there when I was on that Vice Squad investigation."

"What a job!" commented Garry Joplin. "Talk about the little Dutch boy sticking his finger in the hole . . ."

"You're not far wrong. What's on this side? I can't see."

"I thought you might have noticed," Joplin said, "what was next door to this place."

"I was dropped at the door. The next door up looked rather like a brothel."

"No, on the other side—this side, in fact. It's a strip joint called 'Strip à la Wild West.' "

"The mind boggles. Was it," I asked delicately, "wild west girls or wild west boys who were stripping?"

"Girls. Nothing queer about that set-up."

"Not that it makes any difference. I gather you're suggesting that the show would have included guns."

"If you can go by the pictures outside. Guns *and* whips—which sound pretty much alike. If people in the vicinity had got used to hearing them . . ."

"Quite. What's six more shots between friends? Only these were bullets not blanks . . . Of course somebody in the show might have noticed shots that weren't part of the act. I might slip next door and ask a few questions."

"You take all the desirable parts of the job," protested Joplin.

"There is *nothing,*" I said pontifically, "more anaphrodisiacal than backstage in a strip joint. And while I'm mortifying the flesh in that way, you can go along and have a word with Phil Fennilow. He looked as if he was beginning to feel better by the time I left him. He'll probably be able to identify Cordle and the Herbert boy, if he feels up to it, and he just may know the models."

I stood looking around the studio.

"Those bloody cameras," I said bitterly. "Probably clicking up to the second he died, and they're not going to tell us a blind thing. Even if they were sound-recording they probably wouldn't either. Still—get the boys on to developing the film as a matter of priority, will you?"

"Right," said Joplin.

"I'm off to the Wild West."

The Wild West was actually off duty at that particular moment, but it announced its first show for the lunchtime trade at one-fifteen, which was hopeful. One went —as one so often does in these places—down five or six dreary steps, and then came to an improvised box office. The black and white publicity stills on either side of the doors showed girls in various states of undress, but the prevailing motifs were Texan hats, riding boots, holsters, guns and whips. A typical pose depicted a dark-haired model in a G-string, sitting on a stool, Stetson-hatted, with a holster slung around her navel, flourishing a whip above her head. The inspiration seemed more *Blue Angel* than John Ford, but there was something rather half-hearted about the stripper, as if she didn't mean you any harm. No one ever doubted that Marlene Dietrich meant you harm.

I descended the steps to that Soho Hades. The box office was shut, and a locked door stopped me from going further. I banged on it, and after a few moments heard footsteps.

"I'm not open yet," said a voice through the door, which had opened a fraction. "It's half an hour to the show, and my heavy's not arrived yet. Come back in twenty minutes."

"Police," I said, pushing my card through the crack.

"My, you boys in blue do like the boots and whip routine, don't you?" He was being facetious. The door had opened further, and I saw he was a small cock sparrow of a man, formed for being facetious. "Just my joke, Superintendent, though we *do* have the pleasure of entertaining some of your boys in their private capacity from time to time. Colin Burney. My friends call me Col. What can me and my girls do for you? Is it the business next door?"

"Ah, you know about it, do you?"

"Give me credit, mate. Wiv about fifteen police cars having come and gone in the course of the morning, it doesn't take much up 'ere to get the idea that something's happened."

"And do you know what's happened?"

"One of my girls did talk to one of your Detective PCs she happens to be friendly with. All he'd say was 'multiple murder.' Sounds like something the press could work up an interest in. A good story like that can't be bad for trade. Still, I'm surprised it should have happened at Health and Vitality. Not at all good for the old image. Was it by any chance a shooting?"

"Yes, it was. How did you know?"

"Well, most of my girls are here . . . Oh, here's another. Hurry up, Angie—you're late, girl. Don't expect me to lace up your boots . . . Well, as I say, they're down there, dressing like, and they was talking about all this police activity, and Karen said . . . would you like to talk to Karen, though? Hear it from her in her own words, like?"

"I would, yes."

"Anything to oblige the law. You never know when they might come in handy. Karen, love!"

The cry was taken up by female voices behind another door, and after a minute or two Karen appeared. She looked about as much like a Scandinavian as Ingrid Bergman looked like a Spanish peasant in *For Whom the Bell Tolls*. She was raven-haired, fleshy, and heavily made up. Any touch of Scandinavian there had been in her life had been from Norwegian sailors. Still, she seemed a willing enough girl, if several years older than her photograph outside the place had suggested.

"Yes, well, like I was just telling the girls, it was last night," she said, clutching around her an off-white dressing-gown stained all over with stage make-up. "It was the six-fifteen performance, and I'd done my opening routine . . . You haven't seen the show, I suppose?"

"Not yet," I said.

"Well, I'd better explain," she said, putting her hands on her ample hips and thrusting out her bosom professionally. "I start the show with a long routine on my stool—like the pic outside. Lots of shooting and whip-

cracking and that, and quite artistic, though I do say it
myself. Then I go off and the others come on—*filling
in,*" she hissed, *sotto voce,* for the doorway through
which she had come was filled with dressing-gowned
drabs, who were listening to the recital with what I took
to be the lethargy of their tribe. "They do various acts in
ones and twos, and I don't come on till the finarly. That
gives me time for a fag, to adjust my make-up, and put
on my costume, which is a fringed suede Annie Oakley
sort of skirt—all fringe, actually, and nothing on under-
neath. Then I come on for the big number that ends the
show, with all of us on stage, and me in the centre
twirling the whip over everyone's head, and them all
firing shots around the room—the theatre—and all of us
singing, and the pianist wishing he'd got a few extra
fingers. It's a cracking number."

"I can imagine," I said.

"Anyway, that starts about twenty to. Well, last night
I'd finished my fag, and was adjusting my costume—I
think it's very important that it *is* well adjusted—when I
heard these shots, and I thought 'That's funny,' because
there isn't any shooting in the middle part of the show.
It can get too much if you have it all the time, you see."

"What time would this be?"

"Well, see, I'd normally go on for the finarly about
twenty to. But last night Colin here—" Colin, by her
side, smirked—"come running along to say that Bet had
forgotten to put on her raw-hide bra, silly cow, and as a
consequence her strip was three minutes shorter than
usual, and the pianist was cursing blue murder, and I'd
be on in half a minute. So I dashed off, and soon, what
with all the shooting and stuff *on* stage, I forgot all about
what I'd heard *off* stage."

"I suppose you would."

"I didn't even bother to ask the girls what it'd been. But I think I half guessed it was outside. I suppose the time must have been . . . what? about twenty-five to seven, or a minute or two later."

"How many shots was it you heard?"

"Oh, five or six. Was that it? Was that what's happened next door?"

"Yes," I said. "I rather think it must have been."

CHAPTER 4

"Strip clubs!" said my wife Jan, when I popped into the flat in Abbey Road for a cup of coffee, on my way from Scotland Yard to talk to Dale Herbert's father. "It's disgusting the way women are forced to degrade their bodies like that. I can just imagine you and your mates having a finger-licking time. Anyway, why aren't there any male strip shows? Why shouldn't *we* watch men taking their clothes off?"

There seemed to be an inconsistency in her argument, but I didn't say so. Even in these post-feminist days it is more than one's life is worth to mutter the phrase "women's logic." More than mine is worth, anyway. I contented myself with saying:

"Actually, there are male strip clubs, for women-only audiences. Would you like me to book you a seat?"

"Ugh. I can't imagine anything more off-putting," said Jan.

Talking to the relatives of murder victims is never easy. This time it was the more unpleasant in that there were so many of them, and because I had already latched on to the conviction that three out of the four had died quite unnecessarily. I had to judge whether conveying this conviction would make things better or worse for the survivors.

Dale Herbert's father was still bowled over by it when I talked to him. He was a large cockney—could have been a Covent Garden porter or some such thing in his time, but he was now retired. His large frame had put on flesh, but evenly, and he was far from out of condition. He was a sad sight, hunched up in his chair, his face in his hands.

"He was the youngest, see," he said at last. "There's others, four others, and grandchildren, but somehow . . . I'd the bringing up of him, after his mother died . . . That was when he was thirteen . . . Makes you feel you've failed, dunnit?"

"As far as I can see, there's no possible blame can attach to you, or to your son. I rather think that what happened was that your son was just *there* . . ."

He thought for a bit.

"Sort of, with no more meaning than if he'd been run down by an articulated lorry? . . . I dunno, it's difficult to think of it like that . . . I never thought for a moment of warning him against this photography lark. I knew he was going to Soho, but it's not as though Soho's

Chicago these days, is it? It's nothing but poncy pop stars and Chinese cooks, so I never thought . . ."

"How did he come to take up with Bob Cordle?"

"Well, he'd always been a keen little photographer, ever since he was a kid, and I always had to tell him there was a world of difference between taking a nice snap and doing it for a living. Which there is. So when he was sixteen, he'd like to have left school, and he did for a time, but there was no work to speak of, only labouring jobs and temporary things that wouldn't lead nowhere, and he thought he could do better than that, and I thought he could and all, so he went back to school and got a few A-levels, and by then he'd heard about this photography course at the City of London Poly, and with me being retired we knew he'd get a full grant, so I pushed him along a bit, and he applied and got in. He was ever so happy about it."

"Was he still living at home?"

"Yes, he was. But you know how it is with kids— sometimes he'd kip down at one of his mates', and he had the odd girlfriend . . . I hate myself for it now, but I didn't think twice when he didn't come home last night."

His expression was so guilt-stricken and appealing that I said hastily, to put him out of his misery:

"Of course. I wasn't criticizing. Do you happen to know how he met up with Bob Cordle?"

"Oh yes. I was coming to that. I never actually met the bloke but Dale told me all about him . . . We talked a lot, being on our own . . . Well, he was in this pub in Soho, three or four months ago it was, with a gang of pals from the Poly—hangers-on of some pop group or other: Whoosh, or Pink Knickers, or some daft name. Anyway, it was round the corner from Windlesham Street, and this Cordle was in there having a pint after one of his sessions. He'd got a lot of his equipment with him, in cases, like, and Dale struck up a conversation because of that, and he took it out and showed him. He was the first professional photographer Dale had met, and he was a very enthusiastic kid . . . a lovely lad . . ." He dabbed at his eyes. "Anyway, they got on like a house on fire. Very nice man, Dale said—he always said that. Give you the top brick off the chimney, he would, according to Dale, and always helping people one way or another. Anyway, the upshot was he said Dale could tag along to some of his sessions if he wanted, and Dale was over the moon. Not for money, you understand, just for the experience. That's how it happened. Dale used to go along two or three times a week. Felt he was really learning the practical side."

"These sessions you mention—did Dale tell you precisely what they were?"

"Yes. There wasn't any harm in them, so far as I could see. You can't shield a boy from seeing a bit of titty, not these days, can you? It was mostly girls wagging their boobs and blokes flexing their muscles."

"There was nothing . . . more?"

"Well, he did other things, this Cordle chap. There was countryside stuff, and buildings, and that. Dale went with him once down to Essex—you know, thatched cottages and all that malarky. Then a lot of stuff for some architectural paper or other. Dale liked that. He loved buildings, specially old buildings. I used to say to him: 'You like the buildings better than the bodybuilding,' and he'd say: 'They last longer.' I think that's what he would have gone in for, photographing buildings . . . if he'd lived."

"And there was never—well, never any hard porn photography in these sessions?"

"Oh no. Never nothing like that."

"And you think he would have told you if there were?"

He thought long.

"Yes, I do. I really think he would've."

I had to respect that. But it didn't stop me keeping an open mind.

"But he was a good man!"

Mrs. Cordle's outburst was at once an expression of complete mystification and a personal protest to the President of the Immortals. When I interviewed her, she had just returned from her mother's, where she had been told the news. Ellen Cordle—Nellie, I guessed, to her husband—was a slim, fresh-looking woman in her late forties, with a faded prettiness that in other circumstances would have been very endearing. Now, though not weeping, she was clearly in pain from shock and sorrow.

"I'm sure he was," I said awkwardly.

"I suppose you've heard lots of bereaved people say that, haven't you?" she said, shrewdly. "Well, I meant it literally: he was *good*. You think that because he worked for a rather tatty magazine, bought mostly by pretty pathetic people, that he must have been a bit like that himself: grubby round the edges—I bet that's how you've got him marked down in your own mind, isn't it?"

I was in fact finding it rather difficult to mark Bob Cordle down in my own mind.

"Not really," I said. "I heard from Dale Herbert's father how enormously kind your husband had been to his son."

"Oh God, that poor lad . . . My husband treated him like a son. We've got a daughter, you know, but she married and went off to Australia . . . Bob thought the world of Dale. But it wasn't just him. He was good to anybody—everybody, even if he didn't particularly like them. I used to tell him he was daft, but I wouldn't have had him any other way. And he used to say that nobody disappointed him twice. If he got paid back in bad coin, that was the end."

"Was he particularly close to the people who modelled for him?"

"That would depend—on whether they were regular models, and on whether he liked them or not. They were a pretty mixed lot, as I suppose you realize—street-walkers, bouncers, some downright crooks. But he never condemned them, not until he really knew them and had tried to understand. And he'd do anything for them if they asked him. If one of the girls was down on her luck and needed publicity stills taken to get agents interested, he'd tell her to forget the payments till she was in work again. They have such a short career span, these body people. One of the men wanted to go into photography when he got too old for the posing, and Bob went to endless lengths to coach him, lend him equipment, and so on."

"As with Dale."

"Right. Just the fact that Dale was so enthusiastic endeared him to Bob. He loved enthusiasm. He hated

the youngsters who don't give a damn, have a shrug-
the-shoulders, take-it-or-leave-it attitude. That's why he
hated all this youth unemployment there is today. He
said it encouraged this horrible don't-give-a-damn philosophy."

"So he and Dale had become really good friends, had
they?"

"Oh yes. He was here a couple of times—when they
went down to Essex together, and then again when Bob
was doing illustrations for a feature on the suburban
semi-detached house, and he said we'd got just as awful
semis around here as anywhere else had, and he did
most of the illustrations from home. Then they'd do
work together at the studio two or three times a week.
Bob couldn't afford to pay him, and he came along or
didn't, just as he liked. Mostly he did, because he knew
he was getting the experience."

"Mrs. Cordle, I don't want to ask this, but I feel I have
to. Did your husband ever do work . . . well, did he
ever stray into the hard-porn side of the trade?"

"No, he never did. I can see that was how your mind
was bound to be working, and I can say quite definitely
that he never did. Naturally he could have, if he'd've
wanted to, and very profitably. There were people
sounded him out. First time it happened he told me
about it, and why he'd refused, and he never budged
from that. He wasn't one to change, my Bob, once he'd
made up his mind."

"I see. Mrs. Cordle, you've been staying at your mother's, haven't you?"

"That's right. She's been poorly, and she's nearly
eighty, and Bob said to go over and be with her till she

was really better. He said he'd be all right. He was very good at coping on his own, so I didn't worry."

"When you last saw him, was there anything bothering him? Anything he wasn't happy about?"

"No. Not that I recollect. The car needing new fuse plugs, that was about the extent of it."

"And he didn't phone you with any worries?"

"He phoned me, to see how I was, see how mother was going on. But not with any worries."

"Would he have done if he'd had any?"

"Well . . . he didn't bring every little thing that vexed him home with him, if that's what you mean. But we both liked to talk things over, if there was anything big. I think he'd have mentioned it if there was anything important. Unless it was something he thought would *worry* me. Then he might not have mentioned it. He was very considerate, Superintendent."

Probably he was. And if it was something big enough to get killed for, then he might very well not want to worry his wife with it, I thought.

Susan Platt-Morrison had shared a flat in Kensington with a girl called Joyce. The arrangement had only been going a month or so, and Joyce could tell me very little about Susan. Yes, she knew she'd done a bit of nude modelling. It was just a way of making a bit of money on the side, because after all a student grant didn't go very far, did it? Susan hadn't thought twice about it, nor been in the least bit embarrassed about it, and why should she be? Susan had liked the good things of life, especially good clothes and exclusive make-up, and that was her way of getting them. Well, it was better than working your fingers to the bone, wasn't it?

Joyce, in fact, was mainly concerned with getting a replacement to share the expenses of the flat, and practically asked me if I knew of anybody. I could see I was going to get little out of her, so I took off for Mummy in the Thames Valley.

Mrs. Platt-Morrison lived in Hordene, which had once been a pleasant country village, and had several post-cardable bits in the centre to prove it. Now it was predominantly a far-flung outpost of Lloyds and the Stock Exchange. The Platt-Morrison residence was stockbroker's Tudor, set in what the advertisements would call extensive lawned gardens. The lawns were finely mown, the beds weeded, the fruit trees pruned and sprayed. Everything in the garden was lovely.

There was a chain on the front door, and when Susan's mother answered it she peered suspiciously out of the darkness inside. I said "Scotland Yard, Mrs. Platt-Morrison," and handed her in my card. She took it away and switched on a light to examine it by. Then she came and took down the chain and led the way into the sitting-room. All the curtains were drawn, and only two lamps on little side tables were switched on. I had to strain my eyes to establish that Mrs. Platt-Morrison was a well-preserved fifty-five, skillfully made up and tastefully dressed for death.

She motioned me automatically to a chair.

"How could she do this to me?" she exclaimed, almost involuntarily.

"I'm sure Susan had no intention of doing anything to you at all," I said. I then went on, as I had with Dale Herbert's father, though with less conviction in my voice. "I'm sure your daughter was the innocent victim in someone else's quarrel. The innocent bystander who unfortunately found herself involved."

But I had misunderstood her.

"How *could* she let herself down by posing for one of these grubby little magazines? After the education we gave her!"

"I think, you know, it was just a way of making a little extra money."

"Oh, I've no doubt about that. But if she wanted money, why on earth go on being a student half her life? It was no use expecting me to supplement her grant. I'm a widow, you know. I was paying enough for her as it was. This government has been absolutely *foul* to middle-class parents, and I can't think why, when we're its firmest supporters. When I'd paid out what they demanded of me, I'd done all anyone could reasonably expect of me."

I think she thought my eyes must be straying around the plush and dark oak of her sitting-room, though in fact I had taken it all in before sitting down. Anyway, she said aggressively:

"I'm not pretending to be poor. But unfortunately *I* think there are certain standards one should keep up. My husband would have expected it. Richard's one aim in life was to see me comfortably off, if he should go first."

I have known in my time many good family men, but I have never known one whose *one* aim in life was to make sure his widow was comfortably off. I thought Mrs. Platt-Morrison must have made it her business to keep this desirable end pretty constantly before him.

"Did you and Susan get on well?"

"Oh yes . . . yes, of course. She always came home

for the summer. Gave up whatever London flat she happened to be in, and took a new one when autumn term started. Of course I loved having her."

"And you visited her in London?"

"We often got together when I went up shopping. We'd meet for lunch, or perhaps take in a play. Though there are so few plays around that one cares to see these days."

"And did you meet her London friends?"

"Oh no. I didn't know anything about that side of her life . . . Perhaps fortunately."

"She was studying in London?"

"Yes, she was doing a Ph.D. under Barbara Hardy. What was it on? . . . Oh God, yes: 'The Fallen Woman in Victorian Fiction.' She was very nearly finished, I believe."

"And you had no idea about this posing work she did?"

She hesitated. Then she realized I'd observed the hesitation and decided to come clean.

"Well, there was this *most* unfortunate thing a few weeks ago, when Mrs. Pashley made this *very* loaded remark to me. She had caught her son—who's at the grubby-minded stage—with this magazine, and she'd taken it from him. And she told me about it, though Heaven knows I've no interest in her son, and then she added—purposely, of course—"Darling, it was so *funny*, because one of the models looked exactly like your Susan."

"I see. Did you take this up with her?"

"Well, yes. I did, actually. I was in town a fortnight ago, and Susan got us tickets for the new William Douglas-Home play, and in the interval I said to her: 'Darling, it's so funny, but Marjorie Pashley confiscated a nasty little nudie rag from her Paul the other day, and do you know she said one of the models looked exactly like you. Isn't it a scream?' "

"And what did she say?"

"She just stood there, cool as you like, and said: 'It probably was me. I do it now and again to get a bit of extra cash.' As if it was the most normal thing in the world! Without an ounce of shame! I could have strangled her!"

Quite unconscious of what she had said, she leaned forward urgently, displaying more emotion now than at any time since I had arrived.

"*Isn't* there some way this could be hushed up? I mean how she died, *where* she died, what she was doing? The shame of this will kill me."

"Mrs. Platt-Morrison," I explained, trying to be patient, "this is a very serious killing. Four people. The press are on to it already, and of course we can't withhold information."

"But can't you just decline to name one of the victims? I shall never be able to face people again. You give children a good upbringing and this is how they pay you back."

I left her in disgust. Of course I thanked her for her help and said goodbye. They expect that of policemen in the Thames Valley.

CHAPTER 5

Which left us with the body whose happy birthday it had been. Joplin, while I was at the Wild West entertainment, had taken Phil Fennilow—who was most unwilling, as if expecting the corpses to rise up en masse and shriek "Thou art the man"—into the studio, and had held his hand while he looked into the model's face. Phil, before he could say anything, went green and ran out to the loo. Afterwards he said he wasn't sure, but the poor chap did have a slight look of Wayne. He himself didn't know Wayne at all well, but he showed Joplin an issue of *Bodies* for three or four months back, and Joplin agreed there definitely was a resemblance. In Bob Cordle's little book there was a Wayne—indexed under W, as almost all the models were indexed by their Christian names—but the telephone number beside it was crossed through, and above it Cordle had written in pencil the one word "Jim's."

"Only there's no Jim in the address book, so we're back to square one," said Joplin next morning to me, as we conferred in my office in New Scotland Yard, both rather bleary from lack of sleep.

"Hasn't Fennilow got any records of him—for payment of fees and so on?"

"Cordle did all the paying, cash. An income tax dodge, I would imagine. All these models were a bit on the fringe—morally, legally, you know what I mean."

"Oh, I know what you mean. Actually, I met a lady at the Wild West whose fringe was her only badge of respectability . . . Have you got a telephone directory there, Garry? Or, better still, a trades directory?"

"What are you after?" asked Joplin, burrowing in a pile of reference material and coming up with a large yellow book.

"Just an idea . . . What would it be under? Gymnasia? Ha! They call them gymnasiums. See under Health Studios . . . Health Studios, see also Solariums. Whatever happened to a classical education? . . . Here we are: Jim's Gym . . . 14A Little Moulson Street. Where's that, Garry?"

"Other side of Shaftesbury Avenue. Not more than a hundred and fifty or two hundred yards away from *Bodies.*"

"Let's give it a try. Two-two-seven-five-four."

"Jim's Gym," said a London voice promptly at the other end of the line. "Can I help you?"

"Yes. I wondered if Wayne was there."

"No. Hasn't been in today, or yesterday. Probably got one of his colds. Is it the modeling? Can I take a message?"

"No," I said. "I rather think I shall have to come round."

We were there in three minutes in the car. Jim's Gym was on the first floor of one of those poky Soho establishments, over a theatrical costumer's that specialized in the sort of costume that is made to be taken off. Jim's Gym, however, seen through its windows from the other side of the street, looked far from dingy—plenty of light, and pinewood on the walls. We went up, and the door was opened by a large young black man, whose muscle was certainly not mere showcase stuff. Not someone I'd care to cross unnecessarily. He seemed friendly enough, though I felt a trifle nervous as I flashed my warrant at him.

"Here, was it you on the blower ten minutes ago?" he asked.

"Yes. Why?"

"Well—" he led the way into the tiny outer office and pointed a large hand at that morning's edition of the *Daily Grub.* The headline was STRIP MAG HORROR SLAYING. That was the *Grub.* They could say it all in four words.

"Why should you think it had anything to do with that?"

"Because of Wayne. He did posing for that mob. I've often taken messages for him. Was it him?"

"That's what we're trying to establish. You said on the phone that you hadn't seen him for two days."

"That's right. I assumed it was one of his colds, or one

of his slight aches. They're right hypochondriacs, some of this mob, and Wayne was—is—one of the worst."

"How well did you know him, Jim—is it Jim?"

"Ha! I should be so lucky! Jim's a myth, or if he exists he sits in an office in the City. We're part of a chain, floated on the Stock Exchange and all that. I'm Charlie. How well did I know Wayne? Well, fairly well on the surface. He was in here most days, though it was only now and again that we'd actually swap more than the time of day. Once they're into their routines they're not really communicable with."

"You could identify him, presumably?"

Charlie grimaced. "You mean the body? I suppose so. It's not something I'm dying to do. Are you sure it's him, then?"

"No, we're not. Do you know if he was going with a girl called Debbie?"

"Don't know anything about his private life, mate. Here, there's people here who knew him a lot better than I ever did. Come along through."

He led the way from the office through into the gym proper. He looked around to refresh his memory as to who was there, then nipped back to get his copy of the *Grub*. While he took it over to a man who was exercising with weights in the far corner, Garry and I had a chance to look around. It was indeed a very light, airy room—light with Scandinavian pine, though heavy with the odour of human sweat. There was all the apparatus I was used to from the Scotland Yard gym, where I had for many years lifted weights, done leg curls and cross-bench pullovers and other such activities—more, I sometimes thought, as a protest against the excessively cerebral nature of my horrible family than because I got any pleasure or profit from it. I still went in for it now and then, but in bursts, and mostly because I had caught a glimpse of my body profile in the mirror.

Mirrors there were a-plenty around the walls here—and even, at one point, on the ceiling too. In them each exerciser could register the sweat, the grimaces of agony, that told him how much good he was doing himself. Some of them, at the end of their training sessions, would no doubt parade in front of them, to admire the improvement in the pecs, lats, traps and delts. Jim's had the whole range of exercise machines—thigh extension, abdominal board, hypertension bench, all that kind of thing, not to mention exercise cycles, all sorts of pulleys, and a dazzling array of weights and dumb-bells. Some of the machines were of such complexity that I could imagine that any member of the uninitiated, suddenly confronted by them, might believe that he had strayed into the sinister inner room of Secret Police Headquarters in some squalid South American dictatorship. Actually some of the effects were pretty similar too.

Because an awful lot of the people procuring new bodies for themselves at Jim's Gym were doing so with gasps, pantings and expressions of sheer agony that in other circumstances might have aroused one's compassion. Jane Fonda, I believe, foolishly advocates workouts until they hurt. Many of these people seemed to be going well beyond that, into some ecstatic state beyond pain. I saw Charlie stop off by some middle-aged type, flabby of body and with a fire-red cherub's face—his mouth open, his eyes gaping, his expression instinct with the torment of it all. What's it all for, I wondered? They still have to fear the heat of the sun. Charlie presumably told him to take it easy, because he gave up the

Seated Chest Press and started doing running on the spot, his eyes straying now and again to the mirror, with its unattractive image of his fat little legs going up and down. Would he, I wondered, go straight on from here to an expense-account lunch?

They were all ages and both sexes in Jim's Gym, but the majority divided themselves into the middle-aged trying to regain form and the young trying to reach peak form. Charlie stopped by one of the latter at the far end of the room who was putting himself through some pretty advanced weight training. He seemed impatient of the interruption at first, but when he stopped to check the improvements in the body part he was exercising by flexing his biceps at the mirror, Charlie shoved the *Grub* under his nose and said something which brought the man out of his routine. He stood there reading for quite a while, and when he looked up Charlie gestured towards us at the other end of the room. They both started towards us.

Wayne's friend, it goes without saying, was a copy-book body, with especially enormous shoulders and biceps like unpleasantly veined grapefruit. His legs were rather short, though, so he looked like an upturned triangle, a sort of human road-sign, topped by a face that was open, well-meaning, but dim.

"Jeremy Greave," he said, in a middle-class voice. "Hi."

"Hi," I said, finding myself in an impromptu bone-crushing contest. "That looked like some work-out."

A slow smile of great complacency spread over his face.

"It's a killer."

"You look great on it anyway."

"Thanks. Thanks a lot." He pointed a finger at the copy of the *Grub.* "You're not going to tell me that was Wayne?"

"I'm not telling anybody anything. I'm trying to find out who he was. I gather Wayne did model for *Bodies?*"

"Oh yes. He wasn't one of their star regulars but he did model for them. When he left his job he put his name down with an agency, and he'd been getting a fair number of jobs recently, among them work for *Bodies.*"

"An agency?"

"For theatrical work, advertising, posing. Anybody who needs a bit of good-looking body—chaps or girls— goes along there. It's run by this guy who was Mr. Southport 1974. The money these jobs bring in isn't enormous, but it keeps body and soul together."

"I see. So Wayne was becoming something of a professional?"

"Just to make ends meet. I do the odd bit myself. And if by professional you mean the mucky stuff, forget it. Wayne was a lovely clean-minded boy. He never went in for that. That I know for definite."

"I see. Do you know where Wayne was—is—living?"

"Oh Lord—let me see. I've been there once . . . he moved there after he left home . . . Cramby Gardens. That's it. Just off the Finchley Road. Bed-sitter, but very large. He's turned it into a sort of mini-gym, of course. He's got a lot of first-rate gear, has Wayne."

"You say he left his job and left home. Why was that?"

"Well, they were connected, really. Wayne was a garage mechanic—had quite a good job in Hendon. But he found that his work got in the way of his training programme. He tried to combine the two, but there was no way he could do it. He was never going to be world class unless he gave it total concentration and commitment. That was what led to the bust-up at home."

"Really?"

"His dad didn't understand that kind of dedication," went on Jeremy, his expression of almost childlike naïveté contrasting with the glistening sweat on his enormous shoulders. "For Wayne his training programme was his way of life. He was working his way forward to a holistic bodybuilding philosophy. His dad just went on about "lazy layabouts"—which was ridiculous, of course —and so in the end Wayne had to leave home. He didn't want to, because he was very fond of his kid sister, but he had no option."

I had an idea.

"His kid sister wasn't called Debbie, by any chance, was she?"

"Yes. I think she was."

"Did Wayne have a girlfriend?"

"A girlfriend? Oh, I don't think so. There were *girls*, now and then, of course, but I don't think there was ever a regular girlfriend, in that sense."

"I suppose it would have interfered with his total commitment to his programme."

"Well, it would really."

"No place for girlfriends in his holistic bodybuilding philosophy?"

"I expect he would have worked out a place for one in time, if he could have found someone with equal dedication. Quite frankly, it's a problem for a lot of us."

"I can see that it must be."

Jeremy was looking round at his weights, drawing a large forearm over his brow. He was itching to get back.

"Well, it's nice to talk with someone who really understands the problems," he said. "Do you build?"

"I dabbled at one time. I think I outran my mortgage limit."

"Do you really think this body is Wayne? Gee—he'll be a great loss to the sport."

"I think it very probably is. Now, there's the question of identifying the body."

Jeremy's massive, top-heavy body backed away, but not, as I thought, in horror.

"You'll have to count me out. I'm in the middle of my programme. If you don't carry the programme through without a break it's practically a day wasted—isn't that right, Charlie? You take Charlie along. He knew Wayne perfectly well."

I'd already decided to do that if I could. As well as the identification, I wanted to chat about the general set-up Wayne was in, and I knew I wasn't going to get any sense out of the sort of person who talks about holistic bodybuilding philosophies. As Jeremy retreated towards his weights and bars I turned back to Charlie, who had raised his eyebrows eloquently at this last exchange.

"Any chance?"

"Oh, I'd do anything for the police. You put my old man away. Still, I need my lunch."

"An apple, a nut and a wholewheat rusk?"

"I was thinking more of a wholewheat steak and kidney pie with two veg, at the Clarendon down the corner." He lowered his voice and said darkly: "Don't confuse me with these dumbclucks, right?"

"What say you go with Inspector Joplin here to identify the body, and we meet at one of the restaurants near to the *Bodies* office in Windlesham Street? We'll stand you lunch in return for a chat, and it'll look better on the expense sheet if it's near the scene of the crime. Say the Greek one a couple of doors down on the other side of the road?"

"You're on," said Charlie. He went over to a youth exercising on the Chest Pulley, and brought him back to man the office. He was a thin adolescent who seemed to bulge in unexpected places—no doubt at some middle staging-position between six-stone weakling and Charles Atlas. Charlie pulled on the top of his track suit, and I saw him and Joplin off in the police car in the street. Charlie by now was quite philosophical about it.

"You won't believe this," he said, as he got in and put the window down to talk, "but though I've seen some bodies in my time, this one will be the first that's dead."

"You surprise me," I said. "By the look of some of those in there I'd have said you would have seen several."

"Are you joking, man? They're all fit men and women. They all make it to the ambulance!"

CHAPTER 6

The Greek restaurant nearly opposite the *Bodies* office was called the Knossos, and its proprietor was Mr. Aristid Leonides, late of Famagusta. I remembered it—and him—well, though I had not actually eaten there since the days of the Vice Squad investigation. I peered through the door into a murky interior and saw that it was half full of men with melancholy moustaches, some of them with their families. It looked like an audition for a remake of *Zorba*. It is said to be a good sign when you find compatriots of the proprietor eating in his restaurant, though I do sometimes wonder if the Greek, Italian, and Chinese restaurateurs don't arrange to eat in this or that restaurant serving their respective cuisines on a turn-and-turn-about basis, to give their places a reputation with the British. Anyway, all these portly men with their boisterous families certainly gave the place atmosphere, and the proprietor, Mr. Leonides, came bustling forward on his little patent leather shoes, beaming and sweating in the way proprietors have. I think he dimly remembered me, and at my request I was shown to the loneliest corner of the room.

"There will be three," I said. Then I took out my identification and showed it to him. "Police. I wonder if I could ask you one or two questions?"

Mr. Leonides studied it for ten or twelve seconds, no emotion showing on his impassive face. Then he said:

"Too high up for licensing regulations. Is it this business opposite?"

"Yes."

"I don't know nothing about that. But just wait a bit. Elena!" He called to his wife, and she came and took over his place near the door. A dark-eyed girl, perhaps just into her teens, came and sat at the cash register, but he shooed her back behind the scenes.

"Is too young," he explained. "We don't want no trouble with the police."

"I'm not aiming to give you trouble," I said. "All I want is any information you can give me."

That, it seemed, was very little. Living in the vicinity of Strip à la Wild West you got accustomed to the sounds of shots, and you certainly didn't notice if the shots came at the wrong point in the hour. Who was to know if they had changed their starting time, or their act? It wasn't the sort of place that *he* would think of patronizing. Yes, he did sometimes stand around the doorway if

business was slow, and yes, he would sometimes have
noticed Bob Cordle or Phil Fennilow, or some of the
models, coming and going across the way. But it was a
quite idle notice, and he couldn't say whether it was
Monday or Thursday he saw them, let alone precisely at
what time.

"Didn't they ever come in here, these people?" I
asked him.

"Sure they come in here, now and again. Not the man
who run it, this Fennilow, I never had him in here, but
Cordle and the models—sometimes together, sometimes on their own."

"Impressions of them?"

"Cordle—he was a lovely man. One of the best. Always friendly, sympathetic, no hassle, no complaints. I
feel real sad about the way he got killed. They must
have been gunning for one of the others. The models?
Some lovely girls. Real lovely. Some a little bit—you
know—tart. But not all. Some real good-educated girls
there was among them."

"I know," I said. "I have a very good-educated corpse
on my hands. What about the men?"

He screwed up his mouth and flung out his hands in a
gesture of skepticism.

"The men, they was a bit different. Some was just
good-looking, like the women, but it's different in a
man, isn't it? And then there was the muscle boys. Always wanting salad with no oil, or special stuff it wasn't
worth my while to go to the trouble of cooking. "What's
in that?" they say all the time—as if I know! You think I
keep track of what's in all these things? My Elena's an
artist, not an accountant. She don't note everything

down, is different every night. No, some of those boys there are a real pain in the neck."

We were interrupted by the arrival of Joplin and Charlie. Mr. Leonides got up with a perceptible sigh of relief, and began bustling them into chairs around my table.

"You gentlemen all police? You all gentlemen from Scotland Yard?"

"I should sink so low," said Charlie, sliding himself into his seat. He did not look happy. I had the impression that if Charlie could have gone pale, he would have.

"It was him" said Joplin. "Wayne Flushing is his name. Or was."

"That was *not* a nice sight," said Charlie. I shoved the menu at him, and he took it to take his mind off the sight.

"Anything?" he asked.

"Within reason," I said.

"Just what is it you want from me for this bribe?" he asked, after we'd all ordered.

"Just talk. Talk about the people at the gym. I'll throw in a few questions now and then, but at the moment I'm at the stage of not knowing exactly what questions to ask. Just chat about the sort of people who come, what they do, how they live, what their problems are. Talk for your lunch."

Charlie sat thinking for a bit as the proprietor fussed around with our bottle of wine. He was obviously trying to get his life-style sorted out in his own mind. When Mr. Leonides went away, he began with himself.

"I got the job because the bosses—the ones in the City, or their underlings—thought the Soho gym was

likely to be a pretty tough place, and they wanted someone who looked as if he might be dangerous in an argy-
bargy."

"And are you dangerous when the need arises?"

"Try me some time when you're not on duty. Of
course I can take care of myself. I've had to. *And* I'll
take care of anyone who doesn't believe it. But the
point is, it's quite unnecessary. With ninety-five per
cent of the customers, there's not a snowball's chance in
hell of their ever wanting to get in a fight."

"And the other five per cent?"

"I'll come on to them later, if you want. I thought you
were interested in the body boys, like Wayne. You'll
have seen today a fair cross-section of our clients. There
are the middle-aged who want to torture themselves
back into shape: perhaps because they fear death is just
around the corner if they go from one enormous business nosh-up to another without doing anything energetic in between, or because some girl or other has
suggested they're not coming up to scratch in some way
or another—anyway, there's that sort of person. And
their fat wives. And some girls with the keep-fit craze:
they're harmless enough, and often quite pleasant. And
then there are the body boys."

"Yes."

"Now, the last thing they want is a bit of barney with
anyone. Might get a bruise, or break their skin some
place, or even strain one of those beautiful muscles.
They're in love with themselves and their bodies, and
their bodies have to be perfect—flawless diamonds.
They are the most docile people on earth. Sheep are
aggressive compared to them."

"You'd think they'd want to use all that splendid muscle-power," said Joplin, apparently mystified.

"They don't want to use it, they want to *show* it. It's like having a fabulous collection of old cars, and never taking any of them out on the road."

"Right. I get the message," I said. "Now, what about them personally? What sort of people are they?"

"Well, you saw Wayne's pal, Jerry Greave. Did he strike you as the world's greatest brain?"

"No. Still, I wasn't expecting all of them to be candidates for *Mastermind.*"

"No. Fair enough. It was the particular *sort* of dimness I was trying to get at."

"Something—*naive?*" I suggested. "Almost simpleminded? That wasn't quite what I'd been expecting."

"That's it. Naive. Silly, rather than stupid. Blinkered." Charlie wagged a big finger in my direction as he began tucking into a plateful of lamb. "Most of them are quite unconscious of anyone else in the world, or any other point of view, and can't believe that anyone else can be less interested in their bodies than they are themselves."

"That sort of tunnel vision can be dangerous. One of the most dangerous things there is."

"That's right. And I could imagine one of them . . . blundering into something. Quite unconscious of the danger. Because they're in a grown-up world without being quite grown-up themselves. Get me?"

"I get you. It sounds right, it sounds interesting. I wonder about them morally."

Charlie made a derisive gesture with his large hands, which were now wielding a knife and fork.

"You mean sex. Policemen always mean sex when they say that."

"Well, let's start with sex anyway. Are they likely to get themselves into anything dubious morally?"

"Well, there are the ones with the Sunday School morality. That's probably part of the never-growing-up thing. Then there are ones who wouldn't even be able to think on that level—their bodies are *all* they think about, and no abstract idea, however childish, can find a footing. And then there's the ones that work out some kind of 'code' for themselves—the code centering around the needs of their training, the cult of the body, the proper use of the little bits of time they have left over from training, diets, contests, what have you."

"Which of these types would you say Wayne was?"

Charlie shrugged.

"Didn't know him well enough to say. Rather on a par with his pal Jerry, I would guess, though perhaps not *quite* so staggeringly naive. I would imagine they both are rather in the personal code category, though what kind of code that would be I'm not sure. It might be a question of what they're asked to do, mightn't it?"

"What *are* these people asked to do?" asked Joplin. I think there was a degree of salacious interest in his inquiry. He had never been connected with the Vice Squad. He still thought there was something glamorous and exciting about the wilder reaches of the sex trade.

"That I don't know all that much about," said Charlie. "Anything I know I've picked up in conversation, and the fact is that the models and the glamour boys don't go in much for conversation. For the models it's a quick workout and off. For the muscle-boys it's practically perpetual workouts, going from weights to expanders to thigh-developers, or whatever. You notice how twitchy poor old Jeremy got, after only five minutes away from it?"

"You've never been asked to do anything . . . dubious yourself, then?"

"No, I have not been asked to flash my prick for the gay mags. If only they knew about me! Actually, I suppose I would do it if the price was right, so I shouldn't be superior."

"That's one of the things they're asked to do, is it?"

"Sure. And the equivalent for girls. The price for that would be quite a bit higher than for any modelling they might do for *Bodies*. Then there's the fladge market—posing with whips and chains and whatnot—open to both sexes, with lots of permutations. Permutations are important in this thing: you've got male and female, straight and bent, and black and white. Then there are the leather people, the rubber people, the child market."

"Are all of those still more profitable?" Joplin asked.

"Don't know. Haven't heard that much about it, frankly. My guess is that it's all that bit too way out—fairly small market, so perhaps not quite so rewarding as, say, the queer picture mags."

"Anything else?"

"Well, films, I believe. Particularly quickies for the video market. Not that I've heard a great deal about them. My guess is that they prefer to employ out-of-work actors. Lots of *them* around, and I'd suspect these model people would tend to be wooden. Ask them to do much more than stand around with a frozen smile on their faces and they'd become an embarrassment. But certainly there *are* porn films being made all the time, and some of the people we're talking about could be involved in them."

"You think any of these people who posed for Bob Cordle would have been willing to do any of these things that you've been talking about?"

Charlie shook his head emphatically.

"No, no. Certainly not. Sorry if I've given the wrong impression. I was talking very generally. There'd be two reasons why most of the musclemen who are currently in the competitive bodybuilding lark would have fought shy of the things I've been talking about. One is that Sunday School morality I mentioned: it would not have been good clean stuff, nor healthy—not even flashing your prick for the gay mags. Most of them might have looked wistfully at the money, but they would have said no."

"And the other reason?"

"Well—another aspect of the same thing. The sport is very conscious of its image. It's used to being thought slightly ridiculous. It doesn't want to be thought sleazy as well. It's a clean-cut, clean-minded, clean-living world, the world of bodybuilding—that's the message. No, anyone who starts appearing in, say, sex films, of whatever sort, is going to get seen and talked about. Someone in the sport is going to go along to one of those little cinema clubs—because not *all* of them are really *that* clean-minded—and the word is going to get around. I don't suppose there is any bodybuilding equivalent of being drummed out of the regiment— your posing briefs being stripped off you at a public ceremony, for example—but I'm pretty sure that sort of activity would do your career no good at all. It would be less dangerous to sell *sex*. What they wouldn't want is to be photographed doing it."

"I get you."

"What these people are concerned about above all is titles, publicity, recognition within their own very small world."

"What you're saying, then, is that by and large these people wouldn't be seen dead—sorry!—pictured in any of the nastier porno publications, or in cheapie sex films?"

Charlie thought for a bit, messing around with the last of his pudding.

"By and large. There'll always be rogue elephants. And I'm talking about while they're active in the championship world. Remember that that's a pretty short life. When it's over, you've still got a lot of life left, and you've got to find something to do with it. I could imagine that some of them would take on anything that was offered them, after their competing days were over. And I could imagine some who would enjoy it, too. What I was talking about was the active and enthusiastic ones."

"Like Wayne Flushing?"

"Oh yes. Wayne was both of those things."

"You mentioned the five percent that you might have trouble with at the gym. I suppose those are mostly the thugs and heavies around the place?"

"Right. And the pimps. Chuckers-out at the clubs, bodyguards to pretty unpleasant characters, types who can be used to lean on respectable citizens, screw protection money out of them. But I don't need to tell you. Obviously you lot have to know the place. Anyway, that type does come into the gym now and then. Mostly they don't make much trouble—not *there*—but trouble is still their business, and it can follow them around."

"Any of them got any connection with Bob Cordle?"

"I thought this Cordle was a *nice* guy," protested Charlie. "Everybody said so."

"So many people say so, that I'm beginning to feel suspicious," I said.

"Well, I never heard of any connection. But then, I never met Cordle. I'm taking his character on trust. Some of them are just plain heavy—a work-out once a week doesn't change that. But there are a few he could have used, though it depends on his priorities: along with the body-beautiful he'd have to take the mug-ugly. They are *not* attractive, these guys, as a rule."

Charlie was beginning to get restive I could see.

"I got to get back," he said, drinking the last of his wine.

"Won't young Anatomy Lesson hold the fort for you?"

"Yeah, but I'll have to hand over part of my wages, and my wages are not high."

I signalled to the proprietor, who was in a huddle with his wife and dark-eyed daughter round the cash desk. The restaurant was now three-quarters empty, the lunch-hour all but over. Charlie had been expansive. I said to him as I settled up the bill:

"Will you keep your ear to the ground? Pass on any whispers?"

"What am I—stool pigeon or Baker Street irregular? I suppose if I *do* hear anything, you know my lunch-hour. But I doubt if I will. They don't talk much, those boys."

"This thing could just be the something that loosens their tongues," I said. "I suspect there are a hell of a lot of frightened individuals. Who might they talk to, if not to other people in the gym?"

Charlie spread his hands out again.

"Wives, loved ones, families? Their agent, if they've got one. Have you got a list of the people who posed for *Bodies?*"

Joplin drew from his pocket the much-fingered red notebook of Bob Cordle.

"Cordle's list, with Christian names and telephone numbers."

"You could do worse than ring around and see if any of them have taken unexpected trips out of the capital. Or if any of them sound shifty—you must be used to judging that. I suspect the first instinct of many of them will be to get the hell out of London, or to lie very low indeed. If, of course, they have anything to hide."

"Good idea," I said. "You've been a great help. Tell me, is it true you've had a soft spot for the police since they took in your dad, or was that just irony?"

"What's irony? Some kind of vitamin supplement? OK, OK, I know what irony is. He was my stepfather, actually. My real dad's identity is a mystery on a par with the *Mary Celeste.* He—the stepfather—used to knock my mother around something horrible. I started weight training so as to be able to take him on, and I was just about to do it when you took him for a case of robbery with violence. That's when I decided, against all the evidence, that the police had their uses."

He raised a hand in farewell.

"*At* times, *in* their place, and provided they don't get in my way," he added.

CHAPTER 7

That afternoon I left the interview with Wayne Flushing's father to Joplin. I felt I had done my bit with bereaved nearests and dearests, and I didn't see that the father, who had apparently kicked Wayne out of the house, was likely to know very much about what his son had been doing recently.

Me, I took Charlie's advice, and got on the phone to all the people who were in Bob Cordle's book, or all of them who were available, which was perhaps about one-third of all the names. Most of the others, I suspected were in the middle of their near-perpetual work-outs if they were male, or on the streets or in the lecture rooms if they were female. With most of those that answered I chatted, or arranged to have a policeman come around at some other time for a chat. There were only two conversations where my policeman's instinct that Charlie had set such store by told me that something might be up.

The first was when I rang a chap who was down in Cordle's book as Vince.

"Is that Vince?"

"Yes. Who's speaking?"

"I believe you used sometimes to pose for *Bodies* magazine?"

A second's silence, and a definite reserve in the voice when he replied:

"I have done, now and then. Who is this calling?"

"It's the police. My name is Trethowan, and I'm investigating the deaths at the office of *Bodies.*"

"I see."

"No doubt you've heard of them."

"Yes . . . Terrible tragedy. Quite senseless. Wayne Flushing will be a great loss to the sport."

The concern that had now entered his voice seemed entirely spurious—an application, like toothpaste on a brush.

"How often have you posed for *Bodies* yourself?"

"Oh, just now and then. Not often."

"You're a bodybuilder?"

"You might say I was . . . though it never leaves you."

"But you still pose? As a profession?"

"Well, I suppose . . . Yes, I still pose as a profession."

"I wonder if I might come round and have a talk with you?"

I had the impression that there were few things that Vince would care for less, but I made an appointment for twelve the next day, and got his full name and address: Vince Haggarty, 52 Dedham Rd., NW2. He said he had nothing he could tell me, which was probably true. It was what he couldn't tell me that interested me. Many people are wary when they find themselves talking to the police, but such a blanket of reserve is unusual.

The other phone call I found intriguing was to a number listed under the name of Denny. It started off unpromisingly.

"They're not ready, and they won't *be* ready till tomorrow afternoon, and that's final, so you can get off my back, right?" said a ripe female voice at the other end.

"I'm sorry. I must have got a wrong number. I wanted to speak to Denny."

"My fault, love. I thought it was Mr. Schomberg, on at me about the blouses. 'E gets very pushy round about this time of the week, and it gets my goat. Denzil's not 'ere, lovie. 'E's gone up to Scotland, to one of them championships. 'E said 'e didn't know when 'e'd be back."

"I'm sorry. I didn't expect him to be away," I improvised.

"No more did I. It wasn't a date 'e'd fixed in advance. It's Aberdeen, and very provincial, and I keep telling Denzil that 'e's in the big time now, and shouldn't bother with this small-time stuff. But a couple of days ago 'e decided, an' orf 'e went up there. I think 'e should save 'imself, personally."

"For the big time?"

"O' course. I mean, look at the titles 'e's won, and the

cups. 'E's been on the cover of *Fitness Monthly*—lovely picture it was, I 'ung it in my kitchen. It made it all wurf while, seeing my Denny on all the news stands."

"I bet it would. I say, would it be possible to come round and have a chat with you?"

"I'm always ready for a chat with someone 'oo's interested in Denny's career. Are you in the training business yourself, then?"

"Only in a small way, very small. Would twenty minutes be all right?"

"O' course. Mr. Schomberg can go whistle for 'is bleeding blouses. It's Twenty Mayburn Crescent, just off the Old Kent Road. You can't miss it."

I parked the police car some way away from the house, then walked up to No. 20 which was part of a brick terrace of houses, most of which had been mutilated by the owners in different ways in the name of improvement. Denzil's mother had had double glazing put in, and a large window in the attic suggested she had got an extra bedroom up there, or perhaps a training studio for Denny. The front apron of garden was a mass of weeds. When I rang the doorbell, the door was soon opened by a squat, energetic little figure in black, who filled the space of the lower half of the door.

" 'Ullo. You the bloke what rang? Come on in. I'm Mrs. Crabtree. 'Ilda to me friends. Would you like a cup of tea?"

"I would indeed."

"Well, come on through. I've got one on."

She led me into a tiny front room, where it seemed that every inch of floor and table space was covered with blouses—finished, tacked together, or merely in parts. Around the room were dummies of both sexes, some of them also wearing blouses over their smooth anatomical anonymities. On the table was a heavy electric sewing machine, warm from use.

"Wait a mo'. I'll move that. Give us a bit of space for the cups."

"Let me do it," I said, gallantly springing forward. "Since your son isn't here to do it for you."

"Oh, I wouldn't let Denny do it. I couldn't let 'im strain 'isself in that way. Anything can happen, you know, when you've got a body as fine-tuned as Denny's is."

"I see. Awkward," I said. I looked to see if there was any irony behind her words. There was not. She let me lift the machine to the floor. Clearly she did not feel that my body was worth the same protective concern.

"Awkward it *is*, sometimes," Mrs. Crabtree went on, fussing around the table. "Any little thing may go— strain a muscle or a ligament, put a joint out, graze the skin. And it *shows* when you're posing. I can see it myself when I go to watch and cheer 'im on. Denny has to be very, very careful. And I'm careful for 'im."

She bustled off to the kitchen and came back with two cups of tea. Then she hopped through the blouses again and returned after a minute with the front page of *Fitness Monthly* for December the previous year. She put it down reverently on the table between us.

"That's my Denzil, o' course. I'n't it a lovely body, eh?"

Denzil, in briefs, was posing with a busty female model over a piece of gymnastic equipment. There seemed to be a total lack of erotic charge between them, considering the acres of bare flesh, but that was no doubt part of the clean image that the body-builders

promoted. Denny, in fact, looked about as *living* as a
Fascist war memorial. I looked from his body to his
mother's: she was resting heavy breasts on the table,
having tucked her stumpy legs under it. Her face was
puffy and veined from drink, but there was a mad spar-
kle in her eyes. When all was said and done, hers was
the body with force and personality.

She misunderstood my gaze.

"Wondering where 'e gets it from, are you?" she cack-
led. "I don't wonder! Mind you, I 'ad a good enough
body in my time. You lose it though, don't you? I know I
'ave. But it was 'is father, really, made Denzil the man 'e
is. Lovely body, 'is father 'ad. Fine figure of a man,
everybody said so. An out-an'-out rotter, mind you, but
a fine figure of a man."

"What did he do?"

"Army. Regimental Sergeant Major. 'Oly terror on
the parade ground. *And* orf, come to that. Couldn't
keep 'is 'ands orf the girlies. I got 'im because I was
preggers with Denzil, and 'e couldn't wriggle out of it,
once I'd gorn to 'is commanding officer. 'E'd wriggled
out from under scores o' times, but 'e didn't get away
from me. Mind you, 'e got his own back, over the years,
one way or another."

"I suppose Denzil admired him?"

"Well, 'e was still quite young when 'e died. I've bin a
widow now nigh on twenty years, praise the Lord. It's
my belief it was the girlies was 'is undoing. Shot, 'e was,
in Cyprus. But all that trouble was dying down by then,
an' it's my belief it was a husband or a boyfriend or a
father wot did it. I always told 'im 'e'd get 'is fingers
burnt one day, but I didn't anticipate that big a corn-
flagration."

She roared with laughter at what was obviously a repertory joke.

I put a step wrong with my next question.

"Does Denny take after his father like that?"

She choked her laughter back, looked daggers at me, and puffed out her cheeks indignantly.

" 'E does *not*. 'E's the cleanest-living boy you could ever imagine. Pure, I'd call 'im. 'E could 'ave 'is pick, o' course: they'd come running the moment 'e snapped 'is fingers, if *I* know women. But 'e don't snap them."

"Why not?"

"Because 'e's not like 'is dad. 'E was a real leering satire, was my Bert, by the end. But my Denzil's got other things on 'is mind. A body like 'is is a precious gift. A terrible responsibility, like owning a piece of fine furniture. You got to live up to a body like that."

She talked of it as if it were a vocation. Maybe she was right. Maybe it was Denzil's substitute for faith.

"So what Denzil spends most of his time at is keeping in shape, I suppose?"

" 'Course 'e does. 'E 'as to. A fine body like that's like a garden: a full-time occupation."

"He hasn't got a job?"

"When would 'e find time to do a job? I earn enough to keep us both. An' o' course he gets a bit of pocket money from the odds and ends of modelling 'e does. There's people as'll pay good money for a picture of a body like my Denny's!"

"I'm sure there are. Who does he model for, mostly?"

"Oh, mostly that poor Bob Cordle from *Bodies*. My Denny's been full-page spread in there more than once. *In* colour. We was both ever so upset at 'im being shot like that. My Denny said 'e was a lovely man. Salt of the earth, that's what Denny said. I never sin 'im so upset as when 'e reads in the papers how 'e'd bin done in."

"Could Denny think of any reason for the killings?"

"No, 'e couldn't. We talked it over, tea-time, when it was in the hevening papers. Went quite white under 'is tan, my Denny did, when 'e saw the 'eadlines. It was like Cordle was a sort of second father to 'im. My Denny was all sort of bewildered. 'E said 'e just couldn't imagine 'oo could 'ave done it."

"Does Denzil model for anyone else, apart from Cordle?"

"Oh yes, 'course 'e does. 'E's got a sort of agent as gets 'im dates—*and* takes a commission on them."

"You've no idea what sort of work this is, who the employers are?"

"Well, it's modelling, advertisements, that sort of thing. Though I've never seen my Denny on the telly. It's been my dearest wish, and it's never happened yet. 'E'd be marvellous advertising muesli, or one of them beef extract drinks, but 'e's never done it yet. I blame the agent. 'E can't be doing 'is job. I'd get on to 'im if I was Denny, but 'e's too shy. Never likes pushing 'isself into the limelight, my Denny."

Which seemed a bit rich, considering that Denny was currently rippling his pectorals for the inhabitants of Aberdeen, and no doubt doing it under the bright lights.

"Did Denny decide to go to Aberdeen before or after he heard of Bob Cordle's death?"

"After. 'E got up from the tea table and 'e phoned 'is agent, and they chewed it over for a bit and 'e decided to go up. 'E said there wasn't any first-rate material going up there, and these provincials got a bit sore if there wasn't anything but the local bodies everyone knew about. What's it to you anyway?"

This last question came out suddenly, and I realized that questions about my interest in her Denny must have been nagging for some time in the background of her mind.

"Actually I'm a police officer. I'm investigating the murders at the *Bodies* office."

She stood up in outrage, and snatched the half-full cup of tea from in front of me.

"A bleedin' pleece officer? Then I tell you what you've done, my lad, and that's got in 'ere under false pretences." (This was uncomfortably close to the truth. Trust a cockney to know her rights and to distrust the police force.) "By rights I ought to complain about you to higher up. 'Stead of which, you can just get out o' my 'ouse this minute. Come on. Beat it."

I began a somewhat nervous and certainly undignified retreat.

"What was your Denny doing on the night of the murders?"

"The bloomin' idea! Trying to incinerate my Denny had anything to do with that! In 'is own 'ouse, too! He was 'ere. All bleedin' day, 'e was 'ere. I can vouch for every minute, because you can 'ear 'is bleedin' bumps when 'is weights 'it the floor o' the attic. Right? Got it? Now get the 'ell out of this 'ouse. Nothing you can do'll make me alter one jot from what I've just said." She opened the door. " 'Op it, copper!"

I didn't believe her, but I was morally at a disadvantage.

"Well, thank you for your help," I said sheepishly.

"I'd've cut me right arm orf, sooner than 'elp you if I'd know you was a copper."

As I retreated up the road she screwed up her face for a final insult.

"For all you're so big, you'll never 'ave a body like my Denny's. Fancy a man o' your age running to fat already."

I imagined the eyes of all the terrace watching me, and assessing my body in relation to Mrs. Crabtree's Denzil's. When I got into the car I had trouble with my seatbelt, so I fear she was right. As I drove off I got on to Scotland Yard by radio and asked for details of the next flight to Aberdeen. There's this to be said for the oil boom. It's made it a hell of a lot easier to get to Aberdeen. If Denny had wanted to get away from it all, he'd have done better to choose Donegal. I found I could drive straight to Heathrow and get on a plane. I wondered whether Denny would have been competing and incommunicado all day. If so, my visit might come, as I wanted it to, as an unpleasant surprise.

CHAPTER 8

The venue for the North of Scotland Bodybuilding Championships was the Alexandra Hall, a minor barn of a place inconveniently far from the centre of Aberdeen. Having clocked into a hotel with breathtaking room prices (one of the less happy consequences of the oil boom), I took a taxi out there, and as there was three-quarters of an hour to go, I scouted round for a bit. It was a hall that looked as if it was used for any and every thing, as the occasion arose, and was therefore probably without regular staff. This did not argue for bodybuilding being in itself a lucrative sport, if sport it be. The rather *ad hoc* nature of the arrangements had its advantages for me, however. I found a door at the back of the hall, and at the door there was no attendant or stage door keeper. I lingered around it for a while, and saw a heavy young man carrying a sports bag wander in. I decided there could be nothing against my doing the same.

Conditions, I suspected, were less than ideal. What the chorus line of an amateur *Hello, Dolly* would have felt about them I do not know, but here we had a collection of very large and fairly mobile young men (and some not inconsiderable young women), and pressure of space was felt, and commented upon. In rooms and corridors they were flexing and posing, smiling he-man smiles and he-woman smiles, and some were having all-over oilings at the hands of friends, a process which certainly made the place seem unbearably small and close. Here and there one encountered the odd, bluff camaraderie, but for the most part they seemed quiet, solitary people, totally absorbed in their own bodies and their preparations for displaying them. At the end of a corridor, in a small room to himself, I saw what I judged to be the best body there: tanned to a suspiciously even milky-coffee colour, beautifully proportioned, and being displayed in all its induced perfection through a series of poses that each seemed to increase the self-absorption of the face above all that muscle. The young man seemed to be removed on to a cloud nine of contemplation.

I recognized the face as that of Denny Crabtree.

I decided to let him be until after the contest, or show, or whatever it was. I turned and edged my way through calves and biceps and pectorals elegantly exhibited, and out into suburban Aberdeen.

Out there things were beginning to hot up. I pushed my way round to the front of the hall again, and through a crowd chatting and laughing and greeting each other. This lot was a good deal merrier than the lot backstage, and perhaps knew each other from sports field or gym. Women were definitely in a minority, but a fair sprinkling of wives and girlfriends there were, some apparently tagging along, others seemingly enthusiastic followers, even cognoscenti. Many of the men were husky enough, but they did not seem to have reached the level of narcissistic self-contemplation of the people inside. I edged my way into the foyer of the hall and up to the box office. It was staffed by a spotty youth, and the seat plans and ticket arrangements seemed improvised and a little chaotic.

"Have you got any tickets?"

"There's no' much wi' a guid view. You're verra late. Och there's one return—a single in row sehven."

"That'll do fine. I'll take it."

So I passed from the tatty foyer into the hall itself, part of a genial, hailing-and-shoving crowd: there were the hearty young men, and their girls, there was a contingent of over-the-hill athletes, there were women on their own—some enthusiasts, some, it seemed, merely making a point—some obvious pairs of homosexuals, some discreet pairs of homosexuals, and the odd lonely man with or without his grubby raincoat. It seemed a pretty good-humoured gathering.

Inside the hall the lighting was low, with lots of coloured spots and a general effect of a disco writ large. It served to camouflage the down-at-heel appearance of the venue, I suppose. If the lighting was low, the music was high—an eardrum-crushing decibel level, doubtless to get us all into apocalyptic mood for the supermen and supergirls who were going to parade before us. I was glad that my seat was well away from the amplifiers. Near would have been unbearable. I located the empty place, towards the end of a row of wooden chairs bolted together just securely enough to satisfy fire regulations, and I slipped past a row of substantial knees and calves to get to it. I sank into it, and wondered whether there had been a programme seller I'd missed seeing, and whether I'd understand the proceedings without.

"Oh, I didn't expect to have a friend with me for the show tonight."

I turned (nervously, if you'll believe me) to my right. It was a short, birdlike man, with frizzy fair hair that looked as if it might be dyed, a sky-blue jerkin, and maroon tight trousers. His face wore a seraphic smile of greeting.

"Good evening," I said, being able to think of nothing better.

"I had a friend with me, but we had a tiff outside, and off he flounced. *Hav*ing got his money back from the box office, which is just *so* characteristic of Pete. Awfully revealing, don't you think? Well, I'm glad he did! It just proves that not all change is for the worse."

I shuddered to think what I was a change for the better from.

"Do you come . . . to these do's often?" I asked, thinking the conversation was beginning to sound like a parody.

"Championships? Oh *yes*. I love them. I was at Peebles only last month, and Dumfries and Glasgow earlier in the year. I know all the Scottish stars, and they know

me! I'll certainly be able to wise you up. You're interested in The Body?"

"Well . . . *Bodies,*" I said. I don't think he noticed
the italicization.

"Aren't we all? Well, we've got a real treat tonight.
There's a Special Exhibition spot by Denny Crabtree.
He's very good—Britain's number four, or five, I forget
which. I've never seen him, so I'm really looking forward to it. His picture's been in all the mags. His pecs
are striated beyond belief!"

"That's a bonus!" I said heartily, to hide my ignorance
of the jargon. "I didn't see his name on the posters."

"No. Only arranged a day or two ago, as I happen to
know from a friend who's one of the organizers. *That*
sold a lot of tickets for tonight, I can tell you!"

At that point the little man, like a peroxided chaffinch, leant forward and said: "I say, I hope you don't
mind me asking, but there's a place some of us go to
after the show . . ."

But the lights had changed to a blaring white spot on
the centre stage, and I was spared from telling him
what I intended doing after the show. The evening's
entertainment had begun.

Inevitably there was a compère. He was one of those
big, over-the-hill men such as I'd seen outside: an Emer-
itus Professor figure, I suspected—someone who had
once been good. He was gabby too, and hearty, and he
introduced the jury and called for a big hand for them,
and he announced the Special Exhibition spot for Denzil Crabtree, and he called for a specially big hand for
him, and we gave them all big hands, and somehow it
was all a bit like being back at a Boy Scouts' concert. I
thought back to Charlie's description of the musclemen

as people who had never quite grown up. Someone ought to be handing round bottles of pop and slices of cherry cake.

After a great deal of gab, the thing finally got started. The first—and longest—part of the show was the preliminary posing for the men in all the various weight classes. I gathered that some weeding out (not the happiest of metaphors, perhaps) had taken place earlier in the day, but it didn't feel like that. In the blinding light one after another came on, to a reverent hush from the audience, to display themselves in a series of seven compulsory poses, each designed to show off a different body part (so my little friend informed me, though the body part in question was so puffed up and thrown at one that I think I could have worked it out for myself). The contestants were a pretty mixed bag, from apprentice figures very like young Anatomy Lesson at Jim's Gym to genuine twenty-stone bone-crushers.

"Lovely," said my companion, of one of these latter. "But to my way of thinking he's not *really* maxed-out yet. He's not got the defi*ni*tion of a real champ."

I shuddered to think what he would look like when he was maxed out, and wondered, too, what he would look like when he was sixty-five, and presumably maxed in again. The mind had simply become numbed by all the explicit yet somehow anonymous physicality on view when round one came to an end. The sign of relief was short-lived, however, for it was succeeded at once by round two, in which one after another they paraded again, this time in more relaxed poses. And this gave way, incredibly, to round three, in which they went through it all again in what my friend told me was the free-posing round—this time there was music, and they each chose the poses that emphasized best their strong points. Back they came, in strict order, to the triumphal march from *Aida, The Merry Widow* waltz, or "You'll Never Walk Alone." It was beginning to become a great drag.

Except that all the swelling and undulating had by now begun to enliven the audience no end. "Show us your back, Lennie," they would shout, and Lennie would oblige with a back like a shimmering oil-slick. "Biceps!" they would call, and up, obligingly, would swell a breakfast grapefruit. I began to judge them by all sorts of irrelevant criteria: their choice of music, whether their smiles were convincing (they very seldom were—mostly they had the strained quality of a New York waitress at the end of a very long day). My friend treated me to a running commentary, apparently believing that I was into all the jargon. "He's just cut to ribbons!" he would whisper, or "He is ripped to the bone!" It all sounded rather nasty, like the chat of slaughterhouse men. Naturally the blonded chaffinch had his favourites.

"Oh, it's Andy MacIntyre," he burbled, when we came to about No. 25 in the over 90 kilo class. "I know him from the gym. You should see him doing his cable crossovers!" I was about to ask mischievously if Andy's hobby was knitting when Birdie went on: "And he's marvellous at these shows. I just love him. He always looks so fit and healthy."

I jibbed a bit at that.

"I should have thought you could have taken that as read."

"But you can't, though. Haven't you noticed? Look at their faces, 'specially when they're waiting to come on.

Notice how drawn they look, some of them. Positively haggard, my dear, in some cases! It's the crazy diets they go in for, and all these steroids. But you don't get Andy doing silly things like that. He's a lovely clean boy!"

After that I looked at the contestants with a new interest, and of course my rinsed birdie friend was absolutely right. (He was also, by now, resting his hand carelessly on my knee, but that's by the by.) Quite half of them did have a strained, unhealthy look about the face which, even when they were on stage, their stretched smiles failed to hide. It was as if the anabolic steroids and the way-out diets bulked up the bodies but drained the face. Interesting.

After the main showing of the men, it was the girls' turn. The compère, by the way, still called them girls, which would have riled my wife no end, but they didn't seem to mind. A new special jury was empanelled, and was duly given a great hand. There weren't a great many contestants, and it apparently hadn't been necessary to weed them out in advance. Apart from the particular sort of posing they went in for, I couldn't see a great deal of difference between this and your common-or-garden Miss World contest, though I was probably missing all the finer points. We were through in no time, and titles were awarded. My friend on my left side relaxed, but his hand had crept further up my thigh. I crossed my left leg over my right. Birdie sighed.

Now it was time for Denny Crabtree's Exhibition. At once there was a renewed air of excitement in the hall. After the compère's enthusiastic Gang Show introduction Denny's tape started, and it was clear that even his music was in a different class. For almost every pose something special was chosen, so that the *March of the Gladiators* merged into *Mars, God of War*, which in turn gave way to "Seventy-Six Trombones." He hadn't quite had it all re-orchestrated for him, as the ice-dancers do, but it had obviously been prepared with great care.

And Denzil himself? I looked first at the face. Even to the most skeptical observer there was no sign of strain or haggardness, only that rapt self-absorption that I had noticed backstage. Presumably, then, he was not knocking back the steroids. And the body under the face? It was undoubtedly splendid. Denzil was not especially tall, by today's standards, but the body was beautifully proportioned, massive shoulders, tapering, with powerful legs and arms. I suppose you could call him a cover boy.

"Look at those cuts!" gurgled Birdie beside me. "That man's got definition."

Yet there was a sense, difficult to put into words, of that body being an assemblage of the best-quality spare parts, rather than an autonomous machine—it was glossy, it was a showpiece body, yet it was somehow blank. And that feeling was augmented by the face, smiling convincingly, yet the smile never entering the eyes, as the music changed from *The Music Man* to *Italian Caprice*, and then to the *Karelia Suite*. And through all that classy stuff Denzil presented us with his back, his front, his right side, his left side, his biceps and his pectorals and that curious blank wall behind his eyes.

"His delts are just phenomenal!" breathed Birdie. "He is so super-ripped it's out of this world!"

Birdie didn't share my doubts, then, and neither did

the rest of the audience. They loved him, and to some extent that love got through to him, penetrated that wall, as perhaps it will with all performers: their love for him tickled his love for himself, and roused him from that self-absorbed dormancy. One could almost imagine that he was purring.

"They really appreciate him coming," said my friend. "Without him there'd have been no one top class."

After Denny had exhibited himself in some final poses—somewhat anticlimatically, I thought, to "I Know I'll Never Find Another You"—we got on to the judging. The long line of hopefuls and hopelesses in the first part had been reduced to five, who paraded again. Finally titles were awarded, including an overall title which went to a local worker in the oil industry—an enormous black who looked as if he could hold up an oil rig without any problems. It was a very popular win with the Aberdonians (the aficionados seemed to have very little colour prejudice, unlike our own dear English football fans), and since he looked the sort of guy who might lift his old mum's sewing machine without making too much fuss about it, it was popular with me too. And so it was with my birdlike friend.

"It's his first major title," he said. "Though of course he's well known to those of us who potter round the gyms. He's a lovely chap. He once refused me, but ever so gently. Now, as I was saying earlier, there's this little place—sort of bistro—where some of us go after the contests . . ."

"Sorry," I said, hoping I sounded convincing, "but I've got this date backstage—"

"Lucky old you!"

"—with Denzil Crabtree."

His face lighted up as some people's will when you tell them that you've shaken hands with royalty.

"You haven't! Oh, I say, you couldn't intro*duce*, could you? I do so admire—"

"Sorry," I said. "This is strictly *à deux.*"

"Oh, I do understand."

And I left him sighing, but sympathetic. He knew all about assignations *à deux*. Personally I didn't quite know what to expect from mine. By the time I had pushed and jostled my way through the good-humoured crowd it was quite ten minutes since the contest had finished. After the atmosphere of sweat and oil it was good to breathe fresh air again. By the back door that had previously been unguarded, there was now a contest official, keeping at bay a little knot of fans. I flashed my identification at him, and he nodded, curious but hiding it well. I passed through into the cramped corridors and little rooms. The muted self-contemplation of the pre-contest visit had now given way to some good-humoured but sober celebration of the local man's victory. He was drinking carrot-juice, and grinning, and propping up the ceiling. But my man was not among the well-wishers.

My man, in fact, was back in the little room that had been made available to him by the contest organizers. And he was back in the same routine of flexing and posing. On he went: calf and thighs; double biceps to the front; side chest, all done with the same silent perfection that he had shown on stage. And all with that same withdrawn, rapt expression on his face, as if he were practising the disciplines of some Eastern religion. One can take so much of that kind of thing, but by now it had become just too much for me. I walked quietly down the corridor, stood in the little doorway, and thrust my identification before his unseeing eyes.

"Police."

The body began the process of relaxing, and the eyes contracted and stared at my little square of plastic.

"Sorry?"

"Police."

His mouth opened, and I was quite sure that the blood drained from his face beneath the beautifully even tan.

"Well, Mr. Crabtree," I said. "What have you been doing?"

CHAPTER 9

Denny looked for a moment as if he was going to faint. He sank down on to a bench by the far wall. I closed the door, hoping for revelations while he was in a state of shock. The little room seemed hardly bigger than both of us. I remained standing, hoping that this would give me an advantage. Because after a moment or two Denzil seemed to collect his wits slightly, and decide to make a fight of it. Mentally, I mean. Denny would never, I felt sure, commit his precious body to any physical fray.

"I don't know what you mean," he said. "I haven't done anything."

His accent was a careful, classless one, middling in pitch, and slightly anonymous, like his bodily perfection. His mother would have said "I ain't done nothing," as no doubt Denny did in boyhood, and still might when his back was against the wall. But now it was that neutral "I haven't done anything." Self-improvement, I thought, cut both ways. At least if he had said "I ain't done nothing" it would have been more truthful. One thing that was clear from his behaviour was that he hadn't done nothing.

"Well," I said, "you react remarkably guiltily for someone who has nothing on his conscience."

"That was shock," he said eagerly. "Coming while I was still keyed up for the Exhibition. And I've never had anything to do with the police."

"Really? Grew up in the East End, hang around Soho, and yet you've *never* had anything to do with the police? That's a remarkable virginity to have maintained that long."

"Who says I hang around Soho? I train in Battersea."

"Well, you've certainly been to the *Bodies* office, to be photographed by Bob Cordle."

"What if I have? Most of us have been photographed for *Bodies*. It's no different from being photographed for *Bodybuilding Monthly*, or any of those mags."

"I didn't say it was. I think you were one of Cordle's favourite models, weren't you?"

He sat thinking, wondering what the best answer would be. It was as if this was a new pose he was holding.

"I posed for him a few times . . . sometimes alone, sometimes with a bird . . . a girl . . . It was all above

board. I don't take on anything my agent doesn't rec-
ommend."

"So you never did anything . . . a bit way out? Bob
Cordle, just to juggle with one possibility, didn't go in
for the small cinema-club quickies? Video naughties?
Nothing like that?"

"No, he did not. You obviously don't know anything
about Bob Cordle. He wouldn't have *touched* that stuff.
Bob was a real gent."

"I'm getting just that bit tired of hearing that Bob
Cordle was a real gent. Every time someone says it to
me, I get that bit more suspicious."

"Well, that's your problem, mate, because it's the
bleeding truth." He drew back as if he had blasphemed
before a Sunday School class. "Sorry."

"So all you ever did for Bob Cordle was pose for him
for *Bodies* magazine?"

"Right. Clothed. Decent, anyway."

"But there is, I suppose, other work around, un-
clothed, indecent?"

Here Denzil patently became more uneasy. It was
interesting to see how much more difficult his lack of
clothing made it to hide that unease. It was a matter of
tensing muscles, which I could not fail to register, but
which shirt and trousers would have covered.

"O' course there is. You know that as well as I do, if
you're in the police. Doesn't mean I went in for it."

"Then you didn't?"

"No . . . Doesn't pay to do that stuff . . . Well, I
mean, it *pays* . . . so I'm told . . . but it doesn't pay
professionally, which is all I care about. Anything a bit
off gets you in bad odour with the powers that be in the
sport."

"Tell me a bit about how you earn your money, then? What sort of thing do you do?"

"I don't really earn that much money. It's a simple life, really. You get sort of devoted to the sport."

"And of course your mother earns."

"That's right, she does."

"Still, what about training equipment, special diets, all those pills and medical aids?"

"Oh yes, sure—those things can cost money . . . Well, apart from the posing, I do advertisements."

"Your mum says you've never been on television."

"No, I haven't, but there's plenty of other kinds . . ." He started up. "Here, have you been round badgering my old mum?"

Quick, this Denzil. I summoned up the courage to push him back on to the bench.

"She was in when I called on you," I said, which was not strictly truthful. "So you've been on posters, pictured in ads in the newspapers, and that kind of thing?"

"That's right. There's a fair bit of that sort of work around. Not as much as if you're a glamour girl, but that's life, isn't it? Unfair. Then there's various sorts of promotional stunts—for the motor show, the boat show, big affairs like that. I don't go much on those games, but they bring in the money."

"Why don't you go much on them?"

"Interfere with training, don't they? I mean, you can spend hours and hours on them, and that plays havoc with your routines. Anyway, they're not serious. What you might call jokey. I'm serious about the sport, and I think it sort of brings it into disrepute."

"Ahh. Now, coming back to the other things I mentioned—the sort of thing that would *really* bring the sport into disrepute—"

Denny turned on his bench and fixed me with his blank, blue eyes.

"I told you, I don't know anything about that stuff."

"You didn't: you said you didn't go in for it. You must know something about it."

"No, I don't."

"No idea who goes in for it, who does the filming, who does the recruiting of the actors?"

"No, honest."

"Come off it, Denny. It's one of the things you boys do. You've only got to pick up the gay mags to know that."

"Then why don't you go along and ask them?"

"I shall, if necessary. Only they don't like us very much there, understandably, and I'd guess they'll be as cagey as you're being."

"I'm not being cagey. I don't know."

"I just don't take that, Denny. Anyway, what I'm looking for is something a bit more serious than a full frontal prick shot for *Fly*. Something quite a lot more serious than that."

Denny squirmed.

"Well, it's no use coming to me."

"What I'm looking for is something that would make a big strong chap like you pack up his bags and fly off to Aberdeen the moment he heard about the four corpses in the *Bodies* office."

"What are you talking about?" Denzil demanded, with an air that approached the self-righteous. "I was giving an Exhibition here."

"No, you *weren't* giving an Exhibition. You're not

even on the posters, except as a last-minute sticker. You volunteered the Exhibition as soon as you heard of the murders. I got *that* out of your old mum—"

"If you've been bullying my mum—"

"It would take a tougher man than me to bully your mum."

A slow, rather silly grin appeared on Denzil's face.

"Yeah. She's got spunk."

"More spunk in her little finger than you've got in the whole of that big body."

"Here—"

"Come on. I want it straight. You practically fainted when I asked what you'd been doing. What was it?"

"Nothing. I told you. You've got it all wrong. Bob Cordle's the last person who'd ever get mixed up in anything . . . dirty."

"Right—forget about Bob Cordle, then. The moment you heard about the murders at *Bodies* you threw a blue funk and fled up here. Now, I'd be quite justified in taking you in for questioning, just on that alone—"

"You wouldn't!"

"—but let's assume for the moment that Bob Cordle was the spotless gent you and everyone else make him out to be. What follows? Here are a couple of possibilities. The reason you panicked was because you were involved with one of the other people who died. Or because you were involved with something 'dirty,' as you so vividly describe it, and you thought it might be raked over in the wake of the *Bodies* affair."

He sat there, thinking—a process that seemed to come harder to him than for Rodin's young man. Eventually, doubtfully, his voice hoarse, he asked:

"You wouldn't really take me in for questioning?"

"Of course I shall take you in, if I think you have anything to do with the *Bodies* business."

"It'd ruin me in the sport."

"What's that to me?"

Hard, Perry, hard! Could you deny poor little Birdie that ecstatic delight that Denzil seemed to arouse among aficionados? Well, yes, I could. Sorry, Birdie: there was no other way. Denzil Crabtree takes some getting through to.

"I'll tell you," he said, finally.

"I thought you'd decide to do that," I said.

"But it won't have to come out, will it? If you find it's nothing to do with the killings—and it isn't, honest!— you can keep quiet about my part in it, can't you?"

"If it *is* nothing to do with the *Bodies* affair, we can probably keep the lid on it," I said cautiously. He seemed to ignore my qualifications, and to be more relieved than he ought to have been.

"I'll tell you, then." He shifted uneasily on his bench, looked up into my face to see what my expression was, and finding little comfort there looked down again at his thighs. "It's a silly business, and it's the only time I stepped off the strait and narrow. Because normally I just take what my agent offers, and he wouldn't touch a thing like that, I tell you straight . . . Trouble is, the things he *does* touch don't bring in all that much money. Being legit and very occasional."

"But you needed money?"

"For equipment. Not having a regular job—just the dole, and Supplementary, and that, and what I can pick up from the odd job here and there—it's a tight squeeze sometimes. Normally I can manage, but there was this new type of lat machine I wanted for my gym in the attic—it was just what I needed, just the thing to put the finishing touches, get me into the ultimate shape, and it cost the earth."

"And you'd been telling people how much you wanted it?"

"Well," he said uncertainly, "I suppose so. Mates at the gym, and that."

"And quite by chance someone approached you?"

"Yes. How did you know? It was quite out of the blue."

"Out of the blue movies, more like. Sorry, I interrupted. Just tell me what happened."

"It was about a month ago. I was coming away from a posing session at an advertising agency's studio in Wardour Street. For some North Country ale, though I never touch alcohol in point of fact, on principle. Well, so I was walking through Soho, and I met up with a mate, and we went for a drink—"

"Who was the mate?"

"Well . . . it was Wayne Flushing, actually. He was coming out of Jim's Gym. But he's got nothing to do with this. Nothing at all . . . Anyway, we went to this pub, because pubs in Soho are often useful, and you can make lots of contacts there—"

"Don't I know it," I said feelingly.

"—and while Wayne was up at the bar, getting fill-up bitter lemons for both of us, this man approached—"

"Someone you knew?"

"Oh no."

"What was he like?"

"Small . . . dark . . . a bit of a paunch." Denny's words had all the air of a slow-thinking improvisation.

"Hmm. All right. Go on."

"Anyway, he said: Did I want to make a lot of money in a dead easy way? And when I said that at that particular moment in time I did, he said wait behind when Wayne went."

"Which you did?"

"Yes. Said I wanted another. I think Wayne was a bit suspicious, because you can have just so many bitter lemons. Anyway, I stayed behind, and this chap, this little chap, came up again, and he offered me good money if I'd take part in this film . . ."

I sighed.

"I see. How much, and what was the kink?"

"Four hundred. And there wasn't any kink. It was straight sex with a gorgeous model, he said. And he said the sex could be . . . what's the word . . . faked"

"Simulated?"

"That's it"

"That must have been a great relief."

"Here, you're not taking this seriously."

"So far it's not a patch on *Sons and Lovers*. Be glad I'm not pigeonholing it with Grimm's Fairy Tales. So you jumped at the idea, did you?"

"No. I didn't. It's the sort of thing you just don't do, if you're in this business."

"So what convinced you? He upped the fee, I suppose?"

"Well, there was that. But I told him I couldn't have my face used. It would be recognized and known, by someone or other in the business. And he said it could be arranged, though he downed the fee again, because of the technical difficulties that would involve. He said this was going to be one of several . . . bits, like episodes, in a film called *Copulations*. And this one they would shoot mostly from behind, or cut it off at the neck if they used front shots—see what I mean?"

"Oh yes. That was the expendable bit of you."

"Well, yes," he said, looking up at me again, doubtfully. I don't think Denny appreciated me. "Anyway, I made more conditions, like that I wanted to know as little about the thing as possible. I said I wanted to be taken to the studio in a blindfold, and that."

"Why on earth did you stipulate that?"

"I just wanted to know as little as possible about it. Just . . . do it, like, and take the money and go. I mean, just in case someone thought they recognized my body —because it's very well-known—and officials of the sport started asking questions. They can catch you out, can't they?"

"I should think it very likely they could. You didn't specify that the cameramen should be blindfolded too?"

"No, I didn't think of that," he said regretfully.

"Anyway, you did it?"

"Yes, I did. I wish to hell . . . sorry . . . I wish I never had. They picked me up at home, put on a blindfold in the car, and took me to the studio. There was just this chap I'd met in the pub—he was sort of director— and one cameraman, and this girl, or rather woman . . ."

"You recognized her? She was the girl who was killed?"

"No. That wasn't her. The report said she had light brown hair, and this girl had dark brown hair."

"These things can be arranged."

"It wasn't her. There was a picture in the paper, and it wasn't the girl. This girl was sort of . . . tartish. Common—know what I mean? . . . Anyway, we took our clothes off, and . . . and this bloke directed it all . . . and we sort of did it. It was all stimulated, like you said."

"Simulated"

"Right. But I didn't like it at all, even so. I mean, I felt it was sort of beneath me. I just did what he told me and thought of that lat machine."

"Mrs. Stanley Baldwin would probably have approved."

"Who's she?"

"She is said to have recommended shutting one's eyes and thinking of England."

"Was she in these films?"

"I think I can say quite categorically, no. So, when the film, or the episode, was in the can, you put the blindfold on again and they took you home?"

"That's right."

"And that's it, is it? Story over?"

"Well, I thought it was. Hoped it was. I don't know why you're so cynical about it. That's what happened."

"Cynical? I'm not cynical. It's a jolly good story. I just have the idea that something has been left out."

"I haven't left nothing out, honest." Denny's face showed consternation, and his grammar slipped. "I've told you everything."

"Oh no, I don't think so. Because nothing that you've told me so far explains why, when you saw the story of the *Bodies* murders in the papers, you upped and fled to Aberdeen."

He looked up at me from his seat on the bench, and I put on my most inexorable expression. His eyes once more went down to a contemplation of his nether extremities, and he stayed for some minutes in thought.

"It was just that . . . when I was there . . ."

"Where?"

"Filming . . . in the studio . . . though I'd taken all these precautions . . . I thought I recognized the place."

"Ah."

"See, I'd posed for Bob Cordle, like I said, and though there were classy drapes all around the walls, and o' course a bed, which I'd never seen . . ."

"Yes?"

". . . still, I had the idea that the studio where we made the film was the studio in the *Bodies* office."

"Yes, I did rather think it might be," I said.

Well, it was a jolly good story, as I said. Story being the operative word, because I had the idea that parts of it at least were pure fiction. The point was, which parts? I had a night in the Aberdeen hotel, with a miniature whisky from my room bar whose price suggested it had been brought overland by gold-plated Cadillac from Samarkand rather than distilled in the vicinity, and I had a dawn taxi-ride and the early flight to London to stew the thing over in my mind, sift through the various elements in the story, and fix on the bits I believed in, and the bits I didn't.

It was a real problem. Take the most idiotic element in the whole story, Denny's claim to have insisted on being blindfolded to and from the studio where he had filmed his little bit of porn. Did the idiocy spring from his improvisation under my pressure, or from his stupid attempts to keep himself in the clear even as he dabbled in the dirt? Other elements in his story I was also dubious about. Did he really not know the man who approached him in the pub? Or the woman he appeared with in the film? *Was* it a woman, and was the film really just straight sex? If it was something bent, Denny would be inclined to lie about that. Nothing bent about bodybuilders!

I was back home—such is the wonder of modern travel, that compensates for its discomfort and monotony—for a late breakfast in the Abbey Road flat with Jan and Daniel, our son. Jan was doing translations for various Arabian Gulf embassies at the time, work which mostly could be done at home. Considering the staggering size of their oil revenues, the pay was meagre, but Jan said she enjoyed the work. Of course, over cereals and toast I gave her an edited version of what I'd been up to up North.

"And what was he like, this Denzil?"

"Not too bright. Apart from the one subject of her beautiful son, his mum was a hundred times sharper. I suppose she's been part of the problem with Denny. Everything seems to have fallen away, except the contemplation of his fantastic body—its development, its presentation, its needs. He's become the complete Narcissus. Though perhaps cattle gazing at themselves in a pond gives a better idea of what he's like."

"Yes," said Jan thoughtfully. "You were a bit like that when you were really serious about the weight-lifting thing."

"I was *not!*"

"You were, Perry. You used to spend hours lifting those ball things in front of the mirror in the bedroom, and watching your biceps swell, and wondering whether your pectorals were expanding. It was pathetic."

"What a whopper! There's no mirror in the bedroom, anyway."

"That was back in the Edgware flat, before we moved anyway."

"There was no mirror in the bedroom there either."

I can understand why wives tell lies about their husbands when there are other people present, but I've never understood why they tell them when there's only the husband there. Most certainly there were no mirrors in the bedroom of the Edgware flat. In fact, the only mirror in the whole flat was in the bathroom. I remember I found it awfully inconvenient.

CHAPTER 10

When I got back to New Scotland Yard it was still fairly early in the day, but I found there was someone waiting for me—a girl, pretty, dark, probably in her early twenties.

"I'm Sally Fox," she said, coming with me into my office. "I won't take up much of your time. You may know what I'm going to tell you, or it may not be of relevance anyway."

I sat her down, and she refused my offer of tea or coffee.

"No, thanks. I have to be at Bedford College by eleven. I'm a postgraduate student there, and that's how I met Susan Platt-Morrison, of course. We shared a seminar, and occasionally met while we were waiting to see Professor Hardy. Sometimes we used to get together over a coffee or a beer to discuss our thesis. Mine is on Mrs. Gaskell, and the topics overlapped."

"So you were a friend of hers."

I had said it as a statement rather than a question, but it made Sally pause for a moment.

"No. No, I wouldn't say that. Susan was a very cool girl, almost distant, and very self-reliant. Mostly when we got together the talk was about academic things."

"But not entirely, I suppose, since you're here."

"No. For example, I knew about the posing, how much it brought her in, and so on. She always told you the cost of anything she'd bought, or what anything she'd done had brought her in. Quite coolly, not so much as if she was obsessed with money, rather that it was one of the facts of life it was silly to ignore."

"Not money-mad, but money-based?"

"That's about it. She asked me at one time if I would fancy doing that kind of posing: she said she could introduce me to the right people if I was."

"You didn't take her up on that?"

"No. I said I'd think about it, but I never took her up. I don't know why. I was a bit of a feminist in my teens, and they're very hot on the exploitation angle. Perhaps it was that, perhaps it just seemed a bit grubby. One wouldn't feel too good about the sort of people who'd be looking at you. Susan never brought it up again, but she always talked quite naturally about her own posing, and about the offers she got."

"Offers?"

"Of work, I mean. That was what I wanted to tell you

about. I had coffee with her after a seminar, several weeks before she was killed. She said she'd had this offer —"Real money," I remember she said—if she'd do something that went a bit further than the sort of posing she'd been doing. What the man who approached her had in mind was a short film—"

"Ah yes, I thought it might be."

"A sex film, of course, for the video market. She said there were various proposals—some of them 'a real hoot,' she said. She used that sort of language, though she wasn't upper class, and certainly not of that generation. Some of the possibilities that had been suggested were for pretty kinky films. She said if she did it, she didn't care much either way whether it was straight or kinky. She said she'd just regard it as a job of work, and hope that it wasn't *so* ludicrous that she collapsed with laughter."

"You mean she'd decided to take up the offer?"

"No . . . She said specifically that she hadn't decided. I had the impression, though, that she probably would."

"Is that just because of the sort of person she was?"

"Yes, I suppose so. I didn't dislike her—*really* I didn't —and yet there was very little to like, or to respond to. So hard and cold. I met her once with her mother, at a matinée of *Cards on the Table,* and I think I could guess where the hardness came from . . . And yet she was such a beautiful girl."

"Lovely," I agreed.

"Beautiful," she insisted. "The whole hog. You'd have agreed if you'd ever seen her in life. It sometimes made me wonder. Yeats has some lines about women who, 'being made beautiful overmuch, Consider beauty a

sufficient end, Lose natural kindness—' something, something, something—'and never find a friend.' I felt that had happened with Susan. No natural kindness, no warmth, no ability to make friends, because she had nothing to give. Perhaps it was her family, perhaps it was her beauty, but that's how she was. I think everything was judged quite coolly by her: profit and loss, advantage and disadvantage to Susan Platt-Morrison. If she thought the money made it worth her while going into these films, she'd have done them. It's difficult not to sound self-righteous, but from what she said they sounded a good deal worse than grubby."

"Oh yes," I said. "They'd have been a lot nastier than grubby."

When she'd gone, I went along and found Garry Joplin in the Yard canteen, and had a chat with him about his work of the previous day. The main thing of interest was his talk with Wayne Flushing's father and sister. The father was obviously feeling very guilty that he'd chucked Wayne out of the house, though there was no evidence that this in any way affected Wayne's end. Joplin was convinced that the father certainly had once been fond of Wayne.

"There was regret," he said. "No question."

On the other hand, Wayne had clearly been an exasperating person to have around the house. In addition to the weights and the bars, and the pieces of apparatus that spread from his bedroom to the landing, and gradually took over the first floor, there were the sun bed, the oiling sessions, the depilation sessions, all of them gone into with the utmost seriousness. On top of it all, Wayne was a hypochondriac of the most extreme and old-maidish kind, terrified of draughts, obsessed with pimples, convinced that he was about to catch this or that illness, including many quite uncatchable ones. In the end, and coupled with the fact that after he gave up his job he was a considerable financial drain, it had all got to be too much for Mr. Flushing Senior. He had told his son to go, and he had gone.

Wayne's sister Debbie had painted a much more admiring picture. Wayne had the most fantastic body, she'd been with him to the most fantastic contests, there'd been fantastic pictures of him in *Bodies* and *Bodybuilding Monthly*, and altogether he was the most fantastic brother a girl could have. She'd often gone round to the gym to have a fruit juice with him in a health bar after his workout. What she found particularly horrible about his death was that Wayne hated that sort of posing anyway, and was not much good at it. Competition posing was one thing, and that was a vital part of the sport, but posing for such magazines as *Bodies*, or doing advertisements, was something else again —mere glamour stuff, fashion modelling without the fashion. Wayne hated it, and he wasn't one of Bob Cordle's favourite models because it took so much time and so much film before he got it right.

Wayne's flat, Joplin said, had been monumentally unrevealing. Apart from the inevitable equipment, there was a minimum of personal papers, not a single newspaper or book, apart from muscle-building glossies, and no indication of personality or tastes at all. The man was the body. However, in a medicine chest he had found a formidable array of drugs, both doctor-prescribed and proprietary, and on the mantelpiece a model of the Bodmin Nixie, guaranteed to ward off the palsy. All the doors and windows of the flat were fitted with draught-excluders.

By the time Joplin had told me all this, it was approaching the time of my appointment with Vince Haggarty. I didn't quite know what I was expecting from Haggarty, because I knew that so far I had nothing to go on beyond my own ear for a definite edginess in his response when I phoned him. I wasn't sure how I was going to go about the questioning, and I decided that one way to catch him slightly off guard might be to go a bit early. When I rang on the door of his flat, which was the ground floor of a pre-war detached house in Cricklewood, it was eleven-forty, and there was a long wait on the doorstep before the door opened.

"Sorry. Did I interrupt you? I'm early," I said breezily.

"No, no. Not at all. Come on in," said Vince, and he led the way down the hall into the living-room. I wondered if this was the family home, which Vince had inherited, and divided into flats. The room had bits of conventional furniture, most of it rather elderly, though against the bare walls these were boxes and cases of some kind, covered over with drapes. But I had no eye for the room, or for Vince himself for that matter, because the room was filled by a startling creature in a green robe down to her ankles—a robe of the same ethnic provenance as the covers and drapes elsewhere in the room. She was black—her skin of a dull, matt, total blackness such as I had never seen before. She was also incredibly beautiful, of that classical, arrogant African beauty that makes one feel mongrel and tacky. I had rarely seen anyone so exciting in repose.

Vince, I realized, was holding the door open for her.

She said something—it sounded like a European language, soft, full of liquids and sh sounds, like water lapping against a sea wall. Vince nodded, but I rather doubted whether he understood. The woman floated out, her elegance springing from her large, confident body, not achieved in spite of it. Moments later I saw her sailing proudly along the road outside.

"Sorry about that," said Vince, coming back.

"My privilege. I don't often get to meet such marvellously beautiful women as that. What was the language?"

"Portuguese. Refuses to learn any other language, silly bitch."

"Perhaps with a body like that she doesn't need to."

Vince gave a furtive smile, his eyes sharply on me, as if sizing me up.

"She gets by."

"Girlfriend?"

"Part-time. Communication presents problems. She's from one of these ex-Portuguese colonies. She's beginning to do a bit of fashion modelling—could well get to be in demand. That dull black skin sets off certain colours fantastically. She's going to be in *Vogue* next month."

By now I had managed to tear my mind from the woman, and to get a good look at Vince Haggarty. He was a big man—not particularly tall, but broad, and obviously a bodybuilder in his time. The body, though, had begun the process of thickening: though the shoulders were still powerful, the arms were that bit fleshy, and beneath his casual jersey shirt one could see the heaviness of the waist and loins, the beginnings of a paunch. His face was good-looking, knowing, with thick lips concealing a hideous set of teeth—brown and uneven. I thought I smelt tobacco. Once he had been a fitness man, but he had let things slide.

"Tell me," I said, "what sort of connection did you have with Bob Cordle?"

He motioned me to one of the chintzy armchairs, and sat in the other himself, with an affectation of ease which I found less than convincing.

"Not a great deal," he said, "on the social side. But I've modelled for him a fair bit."

"For *Bodies?*"

"Yes, in the past. If you look at the back numbers, you'll find I was on the cover three—no, four years ago. I was in better shape then—though I could still get it back any time, of course."

"Do you mean that you haven't modelled for him recently?"

Vince replied, rather quickly:

"Oh no, I don't mean that. Bob didn't only do the pics for *Bodies,* you know. He hired that room and did a lot of his own stuff there, different times in the week. He did work for this and that firm. Quite a lot of it modelling of one sort or another. There's work of all sorts these days." He gestured with his hand at a glossy brochure on a side table. "Those underwear catalogues, for example."

I glanced in its direction.

"Would that be one of those catalogues they advertise in the Sunday papers?" I asked. "Men's briefs and swimwear, all beautifully photographed on living models?"

"That's it." He gave another of his knowing grins, all lopsided and man-of-the-world. "All perfectly legit, so far as I know, and they pay well, which is the main thing. Then there's more up-market stuff. My agent's managing to get me into the fashion photography lark."

"But that wasn't Bob Cordle's line?"

"Not in the higher reaches. But he did work for mail order catalogues now and again."

"Tell me, what were your impressions of Bob Cordle?"

He rounded his third finger against his thumb, apparently in a gesture of enthusiasm.

"Oh, one of nature's gentlemen. Everyone will have told you that, I imagine."

"They have. So everything he did would have been straight and on the level, then?"

"I'd have thought so. Though it was all just a job to Bob. He strolled through it all. He could—what's the expression?—touch pitch and not be defiled."

"You had a religious upbringing?"

He smiled wryly, showing those discoloured teeth.

"Irish Protestant. But it didn't take."

"Would you call working for *Bodies* magazine touching pitch?"

He backtracked, but delicately.

"Well . . . not really, I suppose . . . But when you think of the sort of people who take it . . . grubby little hands flicking through the paper to find bodies that they fancy—tongues licking round lips when they come on something they lech after . . . It's not *just* good, clean fun, is it?"

"What you're saying is, it doesn't have the courage of its convictions. You think straight-out porn is in a way more honest?"

He sat back in his chair, again with that appearance of ease.

"I don't know that I'm saying anything. But basically it's all appealing to the same instinct, isn't it? That, and the underwear mags, and down to the real hard-core stuff. And that was the game Bob Cordle was working in, wasn't it?"

"I suppose so. He must have cultivated some sort of detachment."

"That's it. That's what I mean. We all do it—the people who pose as well."

"Did you know any of the people who were shot? The two models, and the boy who was helping Bob?"

"I knew Wayne, of course. We were in the same game. Not much of a model, and perhaps not too bright, but good at the competitions. That girl—Susan Platt-some-thing-or-other: she looked a bit of all right, but I can't remember having met her. Of course, in this game it's sometimes ships that pass in the night. You say hello to a nice bit of tittie, appear on a front cover grinning like maniacs at each other, and never see the girl again."

"And the boy?"

Vince frowned.

"Don't think so. Saw the photo in the paper, of course, but I can't call him to mind. But I had heard Bob had this protégé that he was taking around and training up. That would be this boy, wouldn't it?"

"Yes, that would be him.

Well, we nagged around the subject for ten more minutes, without seeming to get any further, and after a bit—apparently gaining confidence—Vince Haggarty said he *did* have an engagement, and if there wasn't anything else . . . I wasn't too unhappy about Vince gaining confidence, because I clearly wasn't going to get anywhere this time. But I was definitely keeping him in mind for some future investigation. I stood up, and let him usher me out to the front door. In the hall Vince put on a maroon blazer, and when we got to the road he eased himself into a nifty little sports car, and, raising his hand in a wave, drove off at speed.

Before I drove off myself, back to the Yard, I sat for a few moments in the car, sorting out my impressions. With Denny Crabtree I had had the sense of a thoroughly untrustworthy story, almost any part of which might have been untrue. I certainly couldn't say the same about Vince Haggarty. But then the cases were dissimilar: I had caught Denny by surprise, whereas Vince had had good notice that I was coming. He had had time to get a story together—had made sure he could give the impression that there was no *story*, as such, to tell.

Why then, I wondered, was I so dissatisfied with Vince's side of the interview? I went through the unsatisfactory elements one by one in my mind.

Vince implied he was still living from posing. Everyone else gave you the impression that one made a pittance from that kind of posing. Vince, apparently, was doing all right from it.

He'd said—no, implied—that he did posing for the underwear catalogues aimed at the plain-cover homosexual market. Was his thickening body, beginning to run to paunch, really the sort of body they used in these brochures? I could no doubt get some from the Dirty Squad people, but I very much doubted whether Vince would be pictured in any of the recent ones.

Again, he said he was breaking into the fashion mod-

elling branch of the business. His face was handsome
enough, if he didn't open his mouth. His body was impressive still, especially when clothed. But was it the
sort of body designers liked to use to show off their
clothes? Much too cumbersome and inelegant, surely.

Again, his attitude to Bob Cordle was odd. He followed the "nature's gentleman" party line, but he was
apparently quite willing to entertain the notion that he
helped in the making of indecent films. Everyone else
had scotched that notion—whether from interested or
disinterested motives.

He implied that Bob was still photographing him for
this or that publication, but claimed that he had never
met Dale Herbert, who had been trailing around with
Bob for three months and more. He had remembered
most of Susan Platt-Morrison's name, perhaps only
feigned forgetting the last part. Would he, if he had only
read about her in the newspapers? Did he know her, in
fact, much better than he pretended?

No, taking it all together, it did not seem to me that
Vince had quite got his story straight. I decided I could
easily get very interested in Vince Haggarty.

Back at New Scotland Yard I was told that a Mr. Peace
had rung.

"Who?"

"He said you might know him better as Charlie."

"Oh, *Charlie*. What did he want?"

"He says he has a little scrap of information. About
worth a plate of moussaka, he thought."

I rang Charlie, and arranged to meet him in the Knossos for a late lunch at two-fifteen.

CHAPTER 11

Charlie and I met at the door of the Knossos, both of us five minutes late. Inside the lunch-time rush was over, with one, two, or three diners at scattered tables finishing off their coffees. The Leonideses seemed to be in the middle of a family conference, with Mama, Papa, and daughter round a large table with another Greek and a boy who was obviously his son. Probably arranging a marriage, I thought. We felt guilty about breaking up the discussions, but the proprietor came bustling up to us in a lather of welcoming sweat, and soon Mama was in the kitchen. Our order was hardly lavish, but before long we were hunched over basins of moussaka, and sipping a couple of glasses of the house wine.

"I don't know that what I've got is worth even this," said Charlie apologetically.

"Let me be the judge of that. I can downgrade us to a sandwich bar next time if it makes you feel easier."

"Well, see if this fits in with anything else you've been hearing about this business. I've been trying to pick up anything I could, see, but like I said, those guys don't talk too much to me. Too busy, too preoccupied with their routines, and not getting interrupted, and getting the maximum out of their time in the gym, which is not cheap. They say 'Hi' when they come in, they do their work-outs, shower, then they say 'Hi' on the way out. A lot of them are natural solitaries, and if they talk it's to each other. About their training routines mostly, I guess. But I got the idea that these days the *Bodies* murders might get an airing in any chat they might have with each other. I tried hanging round health food shops and places like that, where they might meet accidentally, but I didn't have any luck. Then it struck me that one of the places they do talk to each other is in the showers."

"Difficult to hear."

"Difficult but not impossible. And then, they might continue the conversation after the water's turned off. So I did a bit of tactful reorganization of the gym, with the abdominal board and ladder down beside the showers at the far end. Everybody knows that's one of my *things*. Now, yesterday evening two guys finished their work-outs at the same time, and were showering together—"

"Names?"

"Pete Sinclair and Geoff Tate, but I don't think they're anything to do with this. By the time I got to the

machine they were already on the *Bodies* thing. They
were agreeing that somebody must have been doing
something out of order. 'Something a bit off,' Geoff
called it. They agreed whoever it was must have been
doing it for the money. 'I hear good money's being
offered,' Pete said. Now they'd both finished showering,
so I could hear quite distinctly. Pete said: 'Guys who do
that sort of thing have only themselves to blame. It
spells ruin in this game, and they know it.' Geoff said:
'Wayne Flushing was none too sharp.' And Pete said:
'Maybe not, but his agent would have warned him, so he
had no excuse.' Then there was a bit of silence, then
Geoff said: 'Personally I don't see Wayne as the type at
all. But if he had Todd Masterman as his agent, then I've
wondered before now if Todd is quite the clean, upstanding, nothing-that-isn't-above-board man that he
keeps telling us he is.' "

"Interesting," I said. "Yet *how* they've all been swear-
ing by their agent, as if he were the sport's Archbishop
of Canterbury."

"Well, anyway, the next thing Pete said was: 'I never
heard of Todd offering anything dirty to any of his guys.'
And Geoff replied: 'You wouldn't, would you, with that
image of his to protect? I think he goes about it some
other way.' Well, there was a bit more muttering not
much to the purpose, but that was about it."

"Funny," I said. "You're right—it does tie in with
other things I've heard. They do all talk about their
agents. But so far as I remember they all give them a bill
of moral health as the sole arbiter of what is acceptable.
He's the man who protects their reputations in 'the
sport,' as they call it. Just how many of these agents are
there—ones that specialize in body people?"

Charlie shrugged his shoulders.

"A few. But I'd guess there's only the one big one. That's the Todd Masterman that they were talking about. He's the only one you hear mention of, as a rule."

"I think I'm going to drop by to talk to Todd," I said. "I've no doubt I shall find him a fine, upstanding fellow, full of impeccable moral sentiments."

"His office is Two-sixty-one A Dean Street," said Charlie promptly. "I looked it up. He advertises in the muscle magazines."

I noted the number down in my notebook.

"Thanks, Charlie. That was definitely moussaka-worthy. Do you mind my calling you Charlie? I suppose it's someone's bad joke?"

"Yeah. Who *was* Charlie Peace, anyway?"

"A burglar who killed a policeman. Killing policemen wasn't so commonplace then. I don't think otherwise he was an especially interesting criminal."

"Just my luck."

"What's your real name?"

"Dexter, can you imagine? Forget it. I've got used to Charlie."

I paid the bill and we made our way out. The family conference was over, and the restaurant virtually empty. "Keep your ears skinned, if that's possible," I said to Charlie, and we parted again at the door, he to make his way back to the gym in Little Moulson Street, while I turned and walked thoughtfully towards Dean Street.

Number two-sixty-one A, when I found it, turned out to be a slightly tatty three-storey building, very much in the Soho mould. Among the other name-plates by the door, though, Todd Masterman's still had some of the sheen of newness on it. FORM DIVINE AGENCY, it read. T. MASTERMAN (PROP.) Ho, ho, very classy, I thought. I supposed it had been difficult to think of a name that covered both the male and female bodies that Todd Masterman dealt in. Or marketed might be a better word. One must not go in with a pre-formed attitude of disapproval, however: sportsmen marketed themselves —did they ever market themselves, some of them!—so why not musclemen and glamour girls? They had a product people wanted to see (product seemed the word, after watching some of these men at their training—something artificially produced), so why not make sure that the widest public sees it, why not get the best terms possible for the exhibition of their perfection? Bodies fitted as well as anything into our beautiful current free-market philosophy.

I went up the dirty, linoleumed stairs, very reminiscent of those at the *Bodies* office, found the outer door of the Form Divine Agency, knocked, and went in. The girl at the desk was a bottle-blonde and pouting-pretty, with the busty figure of a "fifties" starlet. She could have co-starred in an early Elvis movie. The room stank of the nail varnish she was slipping into a desk drawer. She looked, in fact, the dimmest kind of temp, but I suppose she was engaged because she consolidated the image of the divine form.

"I was wondering if I might have a talk with Mr. Masterman," I said.

I think she thought I wanted him to market my body, because she looked at me dubiously, then drew the appointments book under her beautiful breasts and began peering closely at it. Too vain to wear glasses, I thought, not well enough paid to buy contact lenses.

"Mr. Masterman *is* very busy these next few days," she began . . .

"Police," I said, and pushed my identification in front of her artificially sparkling eyes.

"Oh . . . Oh, I see . . . Well, I'd better go and have a word with him," she said, uncertain about anything outside routine. She disappeared into the inner room, and I heard low voices for a minute through the door that she had closed. Then she reappeared, smiling brightly the smile of the housewife whose whites have just come up whiter than she would have believed possible, thanks to Schmoof.

"Mr. Masterman will see you now."

He was there waiting to shake my hand. Todd Masterman did very much less for the image of the form divine than his receptionist, and perhaps this was why he kept himself behind closed doors. If he was the agent who had been Mr. Southport of 1974, then he had suffered slippage in the intervening years. He was heavy-jowled, double-chinned, and his whole body had fleshed itself out till it became cumbersome and ponderous, centering on one massive belly that no form-flattering trousers could make look anything but gross. There was a posing picture framed over the mantelpiece, and I had to look twice to make sure it was him.

"You lose it," said Todd Masterman, with no regret apparent in his voice. "Sometimes you lose it quite fast. Won't you sit down, Superintendent? What can I do for you?"

We both of us sat down on either side of his desk. His face, in its heavy way, was a powerful one, and had once been good-looking. But it was marred by thinning hair, a straight, hard mouth, and small, greedy eyes. (Come,

come, Perry: we all know, don't we, that there's no art
to find the mind's construction in the face? Common
observation must have shown you many fine, upstanding people with small eyes . . . Yeah. Henry the
Eighth, for one.) Anyway, what I'm saying is, even if the
body could have aimed at avuncular geniality, it would
have been undercut by the face. Nevertheless, Mr. Masterman was an accomplished performer. He looked interested and helpful.

"Was Wayne Flushing a client of yours?" I asked, deciding to dispense with preliminaries.

"Yes. Yes, he was. Not one of my big earners, or someone I had any great expectations of, but he was on my
books. I was able to get him slots from time to time."

"Such as the *Bodies* job?"

"Oh God, yes. Don't remind me. Makes me feel re-
sponsible."

"What other sorts of things?"

"Oh, the odd advertisement, catalogues, that sort of
thing."

"Would you mind telling me, Mr. Masterman, exactly
what you *do?*"

He sat back in his chair, amply filling, even overfilling
it, and prepared to give me a spiel. He had clearly been
asked this before, by potential clients and others.

"I find fine bodies for people. Advertisers are needing
them all the time, you see. If they want a pretty face to
sell chocolate bars, there's plenty of agencies to supply
those. But if the product has a *fitness* connotation, or if
they want to suggest that it might have, then they'll
come to me. Muesli, or glucose drinks, or slimming
foods—they want the people in the ads to look healthy."

"You don't only deal with musclemen, then?"

"By no means. Anyone with a good healthy body. They don't necessarily have to be stripped, the boys and girls in these ads, though they ought to look as if they would strip well. Then again, it isn't only fitness products that use me. Beer isn't one, by a long chalk, but there's plenty of breweries want to give it a he-man image, so they come along to me."

"I'd guess that would go against the grain with some of the people on your books."

"It does. I have to know my clients, and fit the product to the man, obviously. You can get quite a puritanical type in the bodybuilding sport. For some of them, their body is their religion. You have to handle them with kid gloves."

"Right. That's the advertising side. What about the posing and magazine side?"

"Quite a lot of outlets there, though we're not talking about the same kind of money. Hardly worth my while in itself, but you'd be surprised how often it leads to something bigger. So I act as a sort of liaison between the mags and the boys and girls on my books."

"When you talk about mags, do you include sex mags, gay mags, that sort of thing?"

Todd banged the palms of his hands down on the desk.

"Absolutely *not*. Wouldn't touch them. Ruin my reputation, ruin their reputation. That sort of thing damages them in the sport, sometimes beyond repair. You've no idea how careful they have to be, and since more and more of my girls are in the bodybuilding game too, the same applies to many of them. No, no, no. Never."

"I see." I went carefully, deliberately deciding not to question his assurances on this interview. I wanted to leave him confident he was not seriously involved in the case. "Any other sort of work you'd find for them?"

"Stage. TV. Quite a lot of my people have Equity cards, though none of them has stage training. But if they've got the card, I can get them anything that's going. Often the part doesn't require much more than standing around looking healthy. Or the TV detective may visit a gym, so my people can be going through their paces in the background. Or there are some who can do a bit of rudimentary acting—playing heavies, thugs, and so on."

"Wayne Flushing wouldn't have been one of those, I take it?"

"Good God, no. Wayne passed muster at these competitions; he could put on some sort of Exhibition Performance convincingly enough, but put him in front of a camera and you saw his limitations at once. He could just about smile and flex a bicep at the same time. If you asked for much more, you'd be in for a long session. I shouldn't be knocking one of my clients, but that's the way it was. I'd never have signed up Wayne for any of the big things."

"No question, then, of his doing porn films—without your knowledge, of course?"

"Absolutely not. Even had he been willing (which, knowing Wayne very well, as I did, I can tell you he wouldn't have been), he would just have been laughable."

"Most of the porn films I've seen have been just that —but still, I take your point. They'd use people for preference who needed less direction. Now, to get on, you represent a lot of people like Wayne, don't you?"

Todd Masterman sat back confidently in his chair, the master agent.

"Oh yes—most of the best in the field."

"Denzil Crabtree?"

"Yes."

"Vince Haggarty?"

"Yes, in his time."

"I gathered from him that he still does body posing and fashion stuff."

"Oh yes. Vince still looks fine in ads. I just meant his time in the bodybuilding competitions was over."

"What about the girl who was killed? Susan Platt-Morrison. Did you represent her?"

"No. She'd have been an independent operator, I imagine."

"Which of the people on your books, do you think, would be prepared to go into the porn market?"

Todd Masterman leaned forward, very solemn, as if he were discussing a pact with the Devil.

"Now that depends on what you mean by prepared. We're not all angels in this business, God knows, but we're not all sleazy types either, not by a long way. There'd be some who wouldn't have much objection morally to doing that kind of thing—to that extent they'd be *prepared*. Whether they'd be *willing*, after the lecture I give them when I take them on to my books is another matter."

"Stern?"

"I make it very plain that *I* won't be getting them any offers of that kind of work, that if they do it they'll damage, perhaps finish, their careers in the sport, and that if I hear of them taking on that kind of filth, they can look around for another agent, because I won't be handling them any longer."

"I see. They can't say they haven't been warned. What you're saying applies more to the men than the women?"

"Oh, much more. Quite a few girls are going into the bodybuilding side, but it's a bit of an uphill battle to get them taken seriously. Many of my girls are your normal keep-fit kind, not organized in any way, or into any particular sport. For some of those, pretty much anything goes—though I'd still refuse to handle anyone who got themselves into the porn racket."

This last was a hasty addition, delivered with a touch of self-righteousness that I felt patently laid on.

"I see. Now, though you won't involve your clients in it, you must know something about the porn racket."

"No, I don't. Nothing. I make sure that I know nothing. That way I'm sure I don't hear of anything that I might be tempted to offer to my boys."

"I see. The same applies to the gay mags posing, I suppose?"

"Absolutely."

"But some of your men clients must be beyond the serious competition stage in the bodybuilding lark. I was thinking of people like Vince Haggarty, for example."

"Ye-es. I mentioned that." (Cautiously.)

"What's to stop them, for example, accepting an offer from the blue film people?"

"Nothing, except being taken off my books."

"Why should you object?"

"Because of the grubby name it would give the agency if it was known that that was the sort of thing my clients did. The slightest hint of grime I keep at arm's length. Because if it got around, the really serious, dedicated boys wouldn't touch the Agency with a barge-pole, and we'd lose out badly there. Quite apart from the interest you boys might start taking in us. I may say this is the first time we've *ever* been visited by the police. We've kept our hands absol*ute*ly clean."

"That's good to hear. You say you know nothing about the porn film racket. Have you literally *never* heard of *any* of your clients being approached?"

"They wouldn't tell *me* if they had."

"Why not, if they refused?"

"They know my feelings on the subject."

"How do you imagine they would approach likely people, if they couldn't get them through you?"

"How should I know? I tell you, I know as little about that crap as it's possible to know. Through the magazines they pose for, maybe. Perhaps they'd hear about them on the Soho grapevine."

"Through Bob Cordle?"

"Not if they told him what it was for. He was the straightest bloke in the world, was Bob."

"One of nature's gentlemen?"

"Oh, absolutely. He wouldn't have touched anything in the porn line. He'd have felt like me about that. Straight as a die, he was, and *gen*erous? He'd have given you the top brick off the chimney."???

I sighed, rather as the Devil must have sighed at all those hosannas and hallelujahs during his time among the upper angels. Still, I had to admit that Bob Cordle wasn't the only perfect gentleman and parfit knight around in the body game. By his own account, Todd

Masterman must have run him pretty close. It was quite edifying to learn how right the Romans were about the healthy mind going with the healthy body. Funny I'd never noticed it before.

CHAPTER 12

I drove back thoughtfully to the Yard, where I found, not to my surprise, that nothing of interest had turned up while I'd been away. Garry Joplin was around, having been doing routine slog among Susan Platt-Morrison's circle—slog that had turned up little to the purpose. I decided to take him along on my next call.

"Two always looks more impressive than one," I said, "though whether I'm really going to get anywhere by overawing him, I don't know."

"Overawing who?"

"Phil Fennilow. I've really got very little concrete out of my two blokes today, but I can't delay any longer

confronting him with Denny Crabtree's evidence.
Whether he knew it or not, and I can't make up my
mind about that, the place was being used to make porn
films."

"It wasn't being used to make porn films when they
were all shot," pointed out Joplin, as we drove towards
Windlesham Street. "He was doing perfectly routine
shots for *Bodies.*"

"I don't think that makes any difference. The hard
porn element is part of the equation, whether or no. We
know that one at least of his models had been approached about that kind of work. I want to find out
whether Cordle was doing this with Phil's knowledge—
perhaps with Phil looking after the distribution—or
whether it was a bit of freewheeling private enterprise
on Cordle's part . . . Here we are."

The police had long ago packed up their powders and
pastes and cameras, and had left the *Bodies* office in its
usual state, as a dingy oasis in the multi-lingual bustle of
Soho. By now it was late afternoon, and Strip à la Wild
West was beginning to attract the odd customer, urged
in by a commissionaire-cum-bouncer. Soon the blanks
would be firing and the whips cracking. The stairs up to
the studio and Phil Fennilow's office were grimy, the
lino in places worn through to show the wood of the
staircase. When we got to the top, however, I realized
that all was not quite as usual.

From Phil's office, which I had snooped around on the
first day of the case, was coming the sound of voices, and
then a woman's laugh, shrill but whole-hearted. Phil
didn't laugh—I couldn't imagine Phil laughing—but
perhaps he took the cigarette out of his mouth for a
moment to smile. The tones of the voices suggested

they were old friends, and easy in each other's company. I walked forward and knocked on the door. Phil poked his head round when he opened it, blinked at us through his thick glasses, and then ushered us both in.

"These are the cops I told you about," he said. "This one's the big chief."

The wielder of the laugh was a woman in her sixties, thin to the point of scrawniness, with oranged hair, beaky nose, and red talony fingernails. The general effect, though, was vital rather than horrendous, for her whole body had an electric charge, a brisk humanity, which I had heard coming through the laugh. She was expensively dressed, in clothes that suggested flair if not style. They boldly married purple and green, and the combination made it quite inevitable that you noticed her.

"Mrs. Wittgenstein," murmured Phil.

She shook my hand and Garry's, and noticed immediately my reaction to the name.

"Yes, isn't it ridiculous? I'd never have made a philosopher's wife, and I was born a Cohen. Call me Greta."

"The proprietor," murmured Phil, who seemed to have shrunk into an even less blooming state in his boss's vital presence.

"Ah," I said. "I wondered what the financial set-up was."

"Thought maybe Phil owned it himself, and was coining it in, did you? Not on your life! I'm the one who's coining it in." She let out that laugh again. "I keep Phil on *very* short commons. He'd only spend a rise on more cigarettes. Look at him! Listen to that cough! Can you imagine a worse editor for *Bodies?* I'd give him the sack

and find me some healthy glamour boy to do the job if
he wasn't so marvellous at it."

They seemed to be on terms of affectionate chaff. Phil
took out a cigarette and lit it from the butt of his last.

"Did you start the magazine?" Garry asked Mrs. Wittgenstein. Garry was always interested in people with a
gift for money.

"My late husband. He had a flair for identifying areas
that the big chain magazine publishers weren't serving.
So I've got a whole chain of little mags: *Pigeon* for the
pigeon-fancier; *Seventy-Eight* for the collector of old
records; *Match-Box; Medal*—oh, all sorts of little hob-
bies and things we cater for. Some of them I've started
myself. None of them makes quite as much money as
Bodies, though."

"The nearest thing to a universal interest?" I suggested.

"It certainly seems to knock match-box collecting
into a cocked hat," she agreed cheerfully. "It was my
late husband's idea—or his and Phil's, really. Cooked it
up over a meal at Bloom's in Golders Green—though
poor old Sam was no more Orthodox than I am. *Bodies*
went well right from the start, and gradually it built up
a sort of family audience. I'd be the poorer without it, I
can tell you. Phil and I, by the way, were just wondering
what to do about these—they've just come from your
mob."

She gestured towards the desk. On it were the last
photographs taken by Bob Cordle. I had seen them
before, but I took them up and looked at them again.
This was only a selection. There had been an enormous
number from the session, confirming what I had been
told about Wayne Flushing being a less than proficient

performer in this branch of his trade. Susan Platt-Morrison seemed to get things right by instinct, but beside her, Wayne, as often as not, presented a stodgy or an embarrassed image. He was like an amateur actor who had every physical qualification for the part he was playing but no acting talent. The crucial shots were the last two or three. In these one saw dawning bewilderment, then fear, in the eyes of Susan, even as she held her pose, while Wayne, characteristically slower, seemed to register something abnormal only in the final shot. The second after that was taken, the first shot that killed Bob Cordle must have rung out, Susan must have made that pathetic effort to shield her body, and Wayne started towards the attacker.

"Those are the 'ottest pictures we've ever had," said Phil, taking one up regretfully and shaking his head. "And we can't use them."

"No?"

"No. It would be in terrible taste."

"Terrible," I agreed. "But is that necessarily—?"

"We're not that sort of magazine," said Greta firmly. "Whatever you may think. We're not sensational. If we started in that direction we'd become something entirely different, and we wouldn't keep our old subscribers. If I'd wanted us to become a high-price mucky mag, I'd have gone in that direction long ago. We've always tried to go about supplying this particular market with a certain amount of taste, kept it low-key . . ."

"Some of the readers regard the regular models as friends," confirmed Phil. "They'd 'ate to see us capitalize on their last moments. They'd be disgusted."

"But it's only the last two or three that are sensational in any way."

"Yes, we did think we might use one from early on in the session as a full-page memorial to Wayne and Susan. Do it in style, edge it in black, an' all that. They'd posed for us quite often before, after all. I'd write a tasteful piece about them both, to go on the facing page. I didn't know much about either of them, to tell you the truth, but that sort of stuff pretty well writes itself. There'll be something on the editorial page about the murders, but the rest of the mag will be as usual."

"And what about those last pictures?"

Over Phil's face there crept an expression that combined foxiness and embarrassment.

"We thought we'd sell them to the *Daily Grub*."

Greta Wittgenstein saw I wanted to laugh, so she laughed for me.

"Don't be so mealy-mouthed about it, Phil," she screamed. "Of course we'll sell them to the *Daily Grub!* We'll make the earth. They've already offered three thousand for them, and I bet I can get them up to five! *We* may have to show good taste, but it'll be the day when *they* do." Suddenly she went silent and brushed her hand over her face, as if wiping her merriment away.

"What a subject to laugh about, eh?" she went on, after a moment, "When they're dear old Bob Cordle's last photographs. What a lovely man—a man I'd happily have married, if he'd had the good sense to ask me. If he'd been free I'm not sure *I* wouldn't have asked *him.*"

"What was so wonderful about him?" I asked, feeling that this was one person whose judgment I might trust.

"So warm, and quiet, and kind, and everything for other people, and nothing at all for himself. You don't get many like that these days. It's not a breed that seems to be encouraged. But I tell you, when one does turn up, he warms your heart."

She took her coat from a hook on the door, opened her bag and adjusted her flamboyant make-up, then took out her car keys and prepared to be off.

"I'll leave you three to it. I must be away to Much Sleeping in the Wold."

"You don't live in London?"

"No. I shook the dust of Golders Green off my feet. I got the idea that all that kosher food was looking at me reproachfully. And I thought in a village I'd stand out more. I really prefer to stand out. Hence the move to Lincolnshire."

I thought she definitely would stand out in Lincolnshire.

"Pick whichever shot you like for *Bodies*," she said to Phil. "Above all, make it dignified. Treat it as a crisis for the magazine, and write it as if you were editor of *The Times*. One of the pre-Murdoch editors of *The Times*. As to the new photographer, I don't know anything about that. Pick out two or three, get some samples of their work, and we'll talk it over and perhaps interview them. 'Bye!"

And she clattered off down the stairs.

"Salt of the earth!" said Fennilow, as he stubbed out his cigarette. He was about to reach for another when he was seized by a racking cough, and his hand moved reluctantly away from his pocket. "Straight as a die. You can trust anything she says—including the bit about keeping me on short commons," he added ruefully.

"I'm glad to get the ownership of the magazine straightened out," I said. "I did rather think it was probably you who was stashing away the notes. I gather, though, that she leaves the day-to-day running of the business to you?"

"Oh yes."

"And the letting of the studio, and that sort of thing?"

"Yes, broadly speaking. She'd expect to be informed."

"Did you inform her when you let it to Bob Cordle that the studio would be used for making pornographic films?"

Phil looked very angry, and reached automatically for his cigarettes.

"I've told you before, there wasn't nothing like that. We've got a reputation to consider—practically a family magazine we are, like she said. We'd never 'ave touched anything dubious or nasty. We've been over all this before."

"So we have. Still, the fact is, I'm beginning to get evidence that the studio has been used in the evenings to make films that are far from family entertainment. I think the evidence is reliable."

Phil sat down and drew on his fag.

"I don't believe it. I *won't* believe it of Bob Cordle."

"What precisely was the financial arrangement with Bob Cordle concerning the studio?"

"I've told you. I let it out to him—acting for Mrs. Wittgenstein, of course—certain times of the week. Other days it would be free, so that if we wanted to use it for other photographers (we didn't only use Bob, though he was our main one) we could. While Bob had it, he did what work he liked—some days his own, some days work for us. Anything he took for *Bodies* he sold to us in the usual way."

Was I mistaken, or did I detect the slightest beginnings of an attempt to distance himself from Bob Cordle?

"So on certain days the studio was entirely at his disposal?"

"Yes, or parts of days."

"Wednesdays, for example?"

"His from twelve o'clock on."

"Including evenings?"

"If he wanted it. I don't think he ever did. He finished in the early evening as a rule, and after that it'd be empty."

"You say this from your own knowledge?"

Phil paused, and coughed.

"Well, no. I'm never 'ere at nights, am I?"

"I'm asking you."

"I'm a strictly nine till five man. Or more like nine-thirty to four-thirty. I'm never 'ere at nights."

"Never stay up in town for theatre or cinema?"

"What would I do that for?"

I sighed.

"All right, skip it. What it amounts to is that you just *assume* it's empty at nights."

"Yes . . . Yes. I'd 'ave thought it would 'ave come up in conversation with Bob, if 'e'd been using it regular at night."

"Not if he was using it for something he wouldn't want you to know about."

"No . . . I *can't* believe it of Bob."

"What about props, if the place is used for filming?"

"There's a box-room, with the things Bob sometimes used."

"Including a bed?"

"There's definitely a couch. Sometimes he'd pose one of the girls on it for *Bodies.*"

"Let's have a look."

Phil found the key on his ring, and we went out together. He opened a door on the landing. A musty, dusty little box-room it was, with a great deal of photographic impedimenta, with another pile of drapes, all sorts of frames, doubtless to fix cameras on to, and a sofa —a striped, modern job, that looked rather like an *Observer* Special Offer. Garry and I went in and fiddled about with it. It opened out to form a bed. What is more, it opened out very easily to form a bed.

"Right," I said, leading the way back to the office. "At least we know this place holds the first requirement, if bed films were to be made here."

"Pretty elementary bed films, surely," Garry Joplin said.

"Have you been to these scruffy little members-only cinemas?"

"No, actually," said Garry, looking vaguely ashamed.

"Elementary is what they are. Filmed on a shoe-string, if not a G-string. Anything as elaborate as a *set* is a rarity. This sofa, the chair in there, the fireplace— nothing more was needed. Two or three evenings' filming and he'd have a nice little half-hour porno movie."

"Can I say something?" came the voice of Phil from behind us.

"Of course."

"I've told you I've never been 'ere in the evening, so I can't confirm what you're suggesting, nor yet give it the lie. On the other 'and, I often 'ave to call Bob on the phone of an evening. Arrangements for next day, problems with reproducing 'is pictures. I've *never* rung and found 'im out."

He looked at me triumphantly.

"That's not conclusive," I said.

"He's a 'ome bird, Bob. Ask 'is wife 'ow often 'e was out at night. I bet she'll say once in a blue moon."

"Wives' testimony is not very valuable," I said. But I must admit that little worms of doubt were crawling an inch or two further forward. And suddenly, with those doubts, a question or connection that had been bothering me all day suddenly presented itself fully formed in my brain. I looked at Phil thoughtfully.

"You say—everybody says, till I'm tired of it—that Bob Cordle was the soul of generosity, a top-brick-off-the-chimney fellow, is that right?"

" 'E was," said Phil, almost belligerently. "And if you weren't so bleedin' cynical, you'd accept it, when everybody tells you so."

"Cynicism goes with the job," I said. "I'd have thought it might have gone along with the body trade as well, but it seems naïveté's more the thing there. I marvel how you all manage to keep your innocence. But I'll take the uncynical line for once. Good old Bob was always helping people—right?"

"Right."

"Doing free publicity shots for actresses, and helping some of the bodybuilders who are over the hill?"

" 'E did. Well known for it."

"Including one, I gather from his wife, who wanted to go into the photography business?"

"That's right. It's like sportsmen—it's a short career, and at the end of it you've got a life to lead and a living to earn. This chap Bob helped, 'e was a chap who was on our cover—oh, three, maybe four years ago." Phil went over to a rickety shelf in a corner of the room, and took down a couple of files. "When this bloke decided to go into photography, pro photography, like, Bob didn't regard 'im as a potential rival, not a bit of it. 'E was marvellous to 'im, coaching 'im, selling 'im old cameras cheap, showing 'im all the little tricks. Bob was like that: if you appealed to 'im for 'elp, 'e could never do too much for you. Wait a bit—this is the number . . ."

He took the issue out of the file and brought it over. Smiling out at us, but not showing his teeth, was a large, well-muscled man in briefs, one arm around a blonde in a bikini.

"Vince Haggarty," I said.

"That's right. 'E 'asn't got any of Bob's flair, but of course 'e's got marvellous connections in the business. 'E's one of the people I'm going to suggest to Mrs. Wittgenstein to take over Bob's job."

"As your principal photographer?"

"That's right."

"Will you take a piece of advice?"

"O' course, if it's good."

"I shouldn't," I said. "I really shouldn't."

CHAPTER 13

At long last I was beginning to get the idea, perhaps a delusive one, that the case was making some progress. How these new illuminations were going to help in solving the murder was, however, less than clear: so far it seemed to be more a matter for the Vice Squad than the Murder Squad. My suspicions had transferred themselves from the dead to the living, which in some ways seemed less than an advance: as long as it seemed to me that Bob Cordle was involved in the mucky film lark, it was possible to form several scenarios about the whys and wherefores of his death. If he wasn't, those scenarios had to be discarded, without anything very obvious to put in their place. My suspicions about the living, however, were gaining a degree of substance, and I felt sure that somewhere in these murky waters, among this human flotsam and jetsam, the answer would be found.

So far my reconstruction went like this: Vince Haggarty had been helped to launch himself on a professional photography career by Bob Cordle. This Vince had carefully not mentioned to me, which in itself suggested he was operating at the murkier end of the market. When I had called on him (rather earlier than I had appointed, I remembered) he had covered up the equipment he had in cases around the room with his girlfriend's ethnic drapes and wall-hangings. Bob Cordle's generosity had extended to giving him the run of the *Bodies* studio on days when he had hired it, since he himself had no need of it after early evening. Whatever he may have used it for in the first days of his new career, after a time Vince had repaid that generosity by shooting blue movies there—almost certainly without Cordle's knowledge. He, no doubt, was one of those characters that Bob Cordle, if he found himself let down, would never help twice. But in this case the once had done for Bob. I had by now put aside my professional cynicism and admitted that everyone had probably spoken the truth about Bob Cordle's basic decency.

Thus far my conjecture was fairly confident. I firmed it by ringing Nellie Cordle and hearing from her that Vince was indeed the man whom her husband had helped on his way to a career in photography. She was not sure about loaning him the studio, but she thought Bob might have mentioned that. It would be just like him.

Beyond that conjecture I had various more nebulous

ideas, which I was going to have to test. There was also the interesting question of the position in all this of Todd Masterman. The conversation Charlie had over-heard opened up all sorts of possibilities for that self-proclaimed Mr. Clean. Was he the impresario of the whole thing? Did he merely tip off the film-makers about possible performers? Or was he perhaps quite innocent—the victim, like Cordle, of my professional cynicism, the object of quite fanciful suspicions?

After consideration I put that last possibility to one side: he had conspicuously omitted to mention to me Vince's career as a photographer—had, after an initial hiccup, gone along with the idea of his still making a living from posing. That did not argue for innocence.

The next question was how to find out precisely what they were up to. I needed something hard on them, if I was to get anything out of them about the connection between their activities and the *Bodies* shooting—about which I had only the most nebulous theories. Whatever they were doing, it was doubtless not being done at present at the Windlesham Street studio—would never be done there again. But there was this hungry market of video-owners and shady-cinema-goers, avid for novelty. Maybe there was a lull in their activities at the moment, but they would start up again as soon as they felt safe, I had no doubt. The question was, how best to gain entry to their rather special little world.

I thought about that a lot, and the next morning I rang up Charlie.

"Yeah, sure," he said, to my request for a confab. "The usual place?"

"I don't think that would be wise," I said. "Too public.

Anyway, there might be money in this for you, so I don't see why I should feed you as well. Any objections to coming here, New Scotland Yard?"

"I've been in crumbier joints than that. I can make myself at home anywhere. I'm on till half-past five. Some time around six suit you?"

"Perfect."

Charlie's method of making himself at home when he arrived was to sit on my desk. It was his way, I imagine, of asserting that he was not there as a suspect. He made a slightly intimidating figure, while I told him what I guessed about Vince Haggarty's activities. He took it in very quickly.

"I get the picture," he said, eventually. "What exactly did you get out of this Crabtree character?"

"A mixture of fact and fiction, so far as I can judge. He admits that he made a short porn film—part of a larger one—in the *Bodies* studio. There was all sorts of stuff about not knowing the people involved—real cloak and dagger stuff, which I can't say I believe. According to him, it was a straight sex film, with the sex simulated— or stimulated, as he called it. I'm keeping an open mind as to whether I believe that or not."

"And what about Todd Masterman? Beyond that he seems to be covering up for Vince, and what I told you I'd overheard in the shower, you haven't got much to connect him with all this yet?"

"No. Nothing at all concrete."

"Which is where I come in, I suppose?"

"Bright boy."

I'd been intending to approach the matter obliquely, and had worked out various ploys, but he was too quick for me. He shrugged deprecatingly.

"It was obvious."

"Of course we've got our own people we could use. But I couldn't provide cover for them anything like as good as your cover, which is completely genuine."

"I didn't see anything very remarkable in the body line on the way up here," said Charlie disparagingly.

I got all defensive.

"You've no idea of the talent we can rustle up, to send into the gay clubs. But if you're willing—"

"Oh, I'm willing."

"About payment: we've got special funds for operations like this, depending on how much is involved."

"I should damned well hope *so,*" said Charlie. "Though I admit the whole thing promises to be interesting as well. How are you suggesting I go about it?"

"As I see it, the first thing is to approach Todd Masterman. Say you've heard he acts as agent for people with good bodies. You're not a muscleman, not a competition type, but you look good, and you're black, which is an advantage these days. You wonder whether there's any work he could send your way, in ads, modeling, that kind of thing. Probably you could even run to a bit of acting, if something came up?"

"Sure I could."

"If I'm right about the kind of thing they're going to direct your way, it's not going to be the sort of acting that you need an Actor's Equity card for. Say you've heard about him from some people at the gym, which is true enough."

"What if he's not interested?"

"No harm done, from our point of view. End of operation, small fee paid. But if he *is* . . ."

"Yes?"

"Then try to turn the conversation at some point on to a personal level: about yourself and your interests."

"Why?"

"I want you if you get the chance to tell him about something that you want very much—not to be the first black prime minister, or whatever, but something that involves money. Not fantastic money, but some sort of attainable sum."

Charlie got up, and walked around the room, clearly trying to imagine the interview and his part in it, acting it out, thinking forward to what line he would take.

"Think of anything?"

"I'm not that interested in money, to tell the truth. Things tie you down too much. What I want is an interesting life—which is why I'm doing this for you. The gym is becoming a drag: all those guys and chicks looking at themselves in the mirrors. Still, I can imagine wanting something real bad. Would a good stereo sound wrong, do you think? Or what about a really powerful motorbike?"

"That sounds ideal. All the right macho connotations."

"How do you want me to handle the approach?"

"We're jumping the gun a bit—"

"But I presume that's what you're expecting: someone to approach me with an offer?"

"That's what I'm hoping. Not immediately, that would be too crude, and tie it in too obviously with Masterman. Though when I talked to him and to Haggarty I kept it very general—not a trace of accusation. I think they still feel pretty secure. But in fact, if you *do* get an approach, then we can be pretty sure that Masterman is involved. Well, how do you think it would be best to play it? Fairly cool, I'd say. Take a lot of time to consider it. Drive a pretty hard bargain."

"Do I keep any money that comes my way?"

"If it goes that far."

"I'll drive a hard bargain."

"Say you've never done anything like that before, never even *thought* about it. You've no moral objections, but still, you were brought up a good churchgoing lad—"

"I wasn't," said Charlie. "Still, I know plenty that were . . ."

"Play it by ear: the main thing is not to jump at it. There's few that do that, I'd guess, so they'll expect to do a bit of wheedling and bargaining. Obviously you'll want to know the sort of work that's involved . . . Gradually coming to give them the impression that you're open to pretty much everything, provided the price is right."

"Then getting the details of when and where."

"Right. So that we can make the decision whether we bust them then and there, or let it go for a bit. We may well find their plan is to send you gently down the slippery slope, before they land you up in something really nasty."

"Well, let it ride for a bit, can't you?" said Charlie, with ferocious geniality. "I'm not going to get many chances of being in films."

"Certainly the longer you go, the more information you might come across as to who's involved," I said. "But somehow I don't think you'll find the work quite as jolly fun as you think, after a while."

"By 'who's involved' you don't just mean the actors or models, or whatever you call them, I suppose?"

"No. Though I do want to find out as much as possible about them too. We might find that among them are the willing, like you, and the less willing too: ones who are forced into pretty nasty things for the money, or tempted into them by lies. There's a potential behind it: where the money comes from, how the distribution is handled."

"Whether Todd Masterman is in it, and who else?"

"Yes. And, less important, who is in it with Vince Haggarty on the production side. Very few, I suspect. I don't get the impression that these are productions with any great professional polish, though again Denny Crabtree could be lying about that. The approach to you could be made by Vince Haggarty, or it could be one of his underlings who does it. Have you come across Haggarty?"

Charlie frowned and shook his head.

"Not that I know of, though I've heard the name. Must train at some other gym."

"Or maybe his training period was before your time." I got out the four-year-old copy of *Bodies* which I had borrowed from Phil's office. "This was him in his day. The body's thickened out quite a bit. The best way of identifying him will be by the teeth—terrible teeth."

"Never seen him before," said Charlie. "But I should recognize him. Is that the lot? Anything we haven't covered?"

"Not that I can think of."

"When shall I go along to Todd Masterman's? Tomorrow?"

"No reason why not."

"And how do I report to you? Shall we meet as usual in the Knossos?"

I thought.

"I suppose we could. Windlesham Street is not going to be an area these boys are going to hang around at the moment. Keep in constant touch, by telephoning, or by coming round. Here, I'll write down my home address and telephone as well. As soon as something starts happening, we'll meet in the Knossos, some time outside rush hour . . . twelve, two, or early evening."

"Well, well," said Charlie, turning at the door of my office and cheerily waving his hand. "Into the valley of death. Hope to see you soon."

And that was the last I saw of him for some days.

Those days were filled full enough, but not with things that would be of interest to you. Books sometimes give the impression that a policeman is allowed to concentrate one hundred percent on the one case he has in hand. Would that were the case. He always has several in hand, and he juggles with his time as best he can. Even in a matter so important—and publicity-worthy—as a quadruple murder, other things, other cases, other meetings, intrude. Lots of routine was done on the *Bodies* case by lots of constables and sergeants, while I was giving my mind to these other matters. But in fact we all of us felt as if we were marking time.

It's true I was phoned by Todd Masterman, who said he was writing a letter of condolence to Wayne Flushing's father—a likely story!—and he wondered whether there were any developments. I was guarded and noncommittal, but I made sure we chatted on, and in the course of the chat I loosened up, and let slip a mention of a (mythical) jealous lover of Susan Platt-Morrison's. Todd Masterman could hardly keep the cheerfulness out of his voice from then on. He was convinced I'd let

slip the way my mind was working. It may well be, I
thought, as I put the phone down, that he regards this
conversation as giving him the all clear.

Whether or no, three days later I got the message
from Charlie that he'd had an approach.

CHAPTER 14

I heard from Charlie in various ways over the next week and a half. He would ring from phone-boxes, once he sent a note, and a couple of times he called in at the flat and told me everything in résumé form while horsing around with my son Dan on his shoulders, somehow making the living-room seem very small. What follows is pieced together from all those various accounts.

Charlie called at the Form Divine Agency the day after he had talked to me at Scotland Yard. The Agency seemed to be very much as I had experienced it, though the girl in the outer office was putting on mascara instead of nail polish. Once again she said that Todd Masterman was very busy, but quite by chance it turned out that he *did* have a few minutes when he had finished with his present client. (It is perhaps significant that though Charlie was in there with him for half an hour or more, there was no one waiting in the office when he left.) Charlie sat around, passing the time of day with the dumb blonde, but he didn't get anything out of her, possibly because there was nothing *in* her. Eventually Todd's client came out, a female weight-lifter whom Charlie knew by sight and avoided by repute. After waiting a decorous minute or two the dumb blonde had phoned through (though she could just have raised her voice) to Todd's office to say there was this young man there, and of course she knew he was frightfully busy but *could* he fit him in? Todd, in his graciousness, said he would, and Charlie was shown in.

He sat in the chair I'd sat in, with Todd propping his paunch up on the other side of the desk, and he launched into his spiel. He had heard from the guys at the gym that Todd was a fantastic agent, and put a lot of modelling work their way, and though he, Charlie, was not in the competitive bodybuilding lark, he felt he had a pretty good body that would look well in advertisements, or modelling sports gear or underclothes, and he felt he had a good personality that would come over if there were any small acting parts going . . . In short, Charlie sold himself, as I was sure he would be able to.

Todd Masterman nodded during all this, and looked at Charlie appraisingly. At the end of the spiel he thought for a moment. He told Charlie to stand up and take his shirt off. Then he came round to the other side of the desk, felt his biceps, pinched at his thighs to make sure he wasn't spindle-shanked, and generally gave

Charlie an agreeable sense of being back in the slave market in the deep South. Then he told him to sit down again, and they talked.

"It's certainly true," Todd Masterman said, "that there's openings for a well-built chap like you who isn't a muscleman. For example, say I'm getting models together for a sports equipment brochure: the guy who advertises the weights—he ought to be a body builder; but the guy who poses in the football shorts or the tennis gear shouldn't be. Get me?"

"Sure," said Charlie.

"Same with advertisements for ordinary products. They may *demand* a muscleman. If they do, it's often for a fairly jokey sort of advertisement—unfair on the boys, and many of them don't like it, but there it is. For the general public there's something slightly funny about bodybuilding. More often what they want is a pretty fit-looking individual that the ordinary man or woman can identify with. That's where you might come into the picture. You could well be right for that sort of ad."

"That's what I thought," said Charlie.

"You have the advantage of being black."

"It's nice to be wanted."

"It's a pity the abolition of the Greater London Council has meant a cut-down in their advertising. They were very hot on using the minorities—the ethnic minorities, the sexual minorities, the disabled."

"I'd be quite happy to play a black homosexual in a wheelchair," said Charlie craftily. He swore he saw a flicker in Masterman's eye at that point.

"Trouble is, most of the blacks in the advertisements tend to be cast as graduates and professional people—

doctors and solicitors and businessmen. The whites are the roadworkers and dustmen and dockers."

"Couldn't they have a black roadworker just now and then?"

"No, no. That would be stereotyping."

"Perhaps I could be a very well-built solicitor."

"Anyway, with luck there'll still be some of that sort of ad around, even after the abolition. The various local authorities will get together and promote it. And with the vegetarian and health food fad growing all the time, the demand for healthy, sporty-looking models is constantly on the increase . . . Then there's the pure modelling. You wouldn't object to modeling underwear?"

Charlie shrugged.

"Heavens, no. I wear it, why should I object to modelling it?"

"I just like to know. Some of the people on my books have odd kinds of . . . scruples."

He smiled fatly at Charlie, but left the subject there. He pushed himself back once more in his chair, and they began to talk generally. He asked about Charlie's background, where he grew up, how he had come to work at Jim's Gym, whether that was the sort of work he aimed to do for the rest of his life, what he was interested in. Charlie answered all of this quite truthfully, indulging in a judicious bit of heightening only when he felt it might be useful. The gym, he said, was a good job, he'd enjoyed it a lot for the first year or eighteen months, but now it was beginning to get that bit repetitious.

"A bit lacking in excitement, zing, know what I

mean? I'm beginning to feel the need of a bit of variety, something to add a bit of spice to the everyday."

"I see what you mean . . . And you think modelling might give you that?"

"I think it would. I think I could do it pretty well, too. I'm . . . versatile."

"I'm sure you are. And I suppose the money would come in useful?"

"Money *always* comes in useful, man!"

"What does money mean, specially, to you? What have you got your eye on?

"Well, I'm beginning to feel I need to be a bit more mobile. I live in London, but there's a whole lot of things going on that I miss out on because the bus and the tube are such drags. I've got my eye on a motorcycle. Used to have an old crock, when I was seventeen or so, but it fell to pieces. Now I've got my eye on a Nittachi 500—Japanese job, just out in a new model. That's got real power—it's a real smooth, classy job . . ."

"And so on, and so on," said Charlie to me, when he reported back later. "I did everything except say that I wanted to feel its power surging between my legs."

"You did well to restrain yourself," I said. "Though it's remarkable how much of the D. H. Lawrence stuff people will accept without laughing themselves silly. Was that pretty much the end of the interview?"

"More or less. He clapped me on the shoulder, said he was sure he'd be able to find *something* for me, though I mustn't be too optimistic at first, then he took my home phone number—he'd got that of the gym—and that was pretty much that."

"Was there any solemn warning against getting involved with anything dubious?"

"Sorry—yes, there was. That was earlier. He just said that he wouldn't be recruiting me for anything on the nose, as he put it, and if I'd take his advice I wouldn't go in for it. That sort of thing does you no good in the legit trade, he said."

"Not *quite* so strong as he told me he made it," I commented. "What were your impressions of the man, as a whole?"

Charlie thought for a bit.

"He was very matey, very cheery—hail-fellow, lots of ho-ho laughing, and all that kind of thing . . . But I didn't like him . . . He worried me a lot."

"Oh?"

"There was this slave-market element, like I told you, about the whole interview. OK—I'm black, I'm sensitive to that. But if I'd been white, the slave-market element would have been there. Buying flesh, sizing it up, like he was trading in it. Then there was the man himself . . ."

"What was it that worried you?"

"There was all this laughter, like he was everyone's favourite uncle. But when we did all that stuff about stereotypes, I was pissing myself laughing inside, but *he didn't think it funny*. Wasn't conscious it had a funny side. I found that creepy. I think the only way you could run an agency like that would be if you found the whole business a bit of a laugh. But he is fairly stupid, or at least without a sense of humour, and I started wondering what he was getting out of it. Why he was in that business at all."

After that opening interview, there was a bit of a fallow period for Charlie. But six days later he was called by nail-varnish-and-mascara at the Form Divine

Office, and sent off to stand in for someone whose form divine had been hit by 'flu. It was a television advertisement for a crunchy breakfast food of doubtless minimal nutritional value, but the advertising agency wanted to play up the health angle. Charlie and ten or twelve others cavorted around energetically in front of a number of stunning backdrops, wearing a variety of sporting gears, and Charlie said he enjoyed it very much, except that it was difficult to cavort energetically when carrying a bowl of Corni-munch. Later he did a session for a Hackney District Council poster in which he was supposed to be a sports teacher with a multi-racial class. The fees for these jobs were not large. Todd Masterman, phoning him at the gym, said that everyone was pleased with his work, and he (Todd) felt sure that something else would come up before very long.

In the meantime Charlie did not waste his time. He changed his lunch-time habits, forswore pub steak and kidney pie, and walked through Soho munching a sandwich—not always a comfortable thing to do in November. "I wanted to increase my visibility," he explained. At other times he would sit in Soho Square or Golden Square, reading *Power Bike* or other such magazines, or sometimes he would just loaf around the narrow streets of the area, looking with interest at anything unusual on four wheels or two.

One day, towards lunch-time, a man came into the gym whose face he thought he knew.

"I'm just meeting Harry," he said, and stood around in the office reading the *Daily Grub*. As soon as he had opened his mouth, Charlie had noticed his appalling teeth.

Charlie went on sitting at his desk, going through the

gym's accounts for the previous month. He was conscious of eyes on him. Now and then, for verisimilitude, Vince Haggarty would turn over a page of the *Grub*. It was the day on which that journal of opinion printed Bob Cordle's final pictures, the chronicle of the last few seconds of Susan Platt-Morrison and Wayne Flushing. Charlie noticed that Vince turned over that page very quickly. Not natural, thought Charlie, in one who was part of the body business himself. Before long Harry (a rather sleazy young man, not rated serious enough by other people in the body trade) came out of the showers, and the two went off together.

It was two days later, in the lunch-hour, that the approach was made. Charlie had just handed over Jim's Gym to young Anatomy Lesson, and was strolling along Wardour Street, *Power Bike* rolled up in his hand, wondering whether to slip into a sandwich bar or risk a pub lasagne, when he saw a Nittachi 500 leant up against the wall of one of the various film company's offices. Automatically, by now, he stopped to admire it—stood back to wonder at the shape and the sheen, bent down to look at the gears and the speedo, and was just straightening up when he was conscious of a presence behind him.

"That's some machine," said a voice.

"Yes, man!" said Charlie, with joyous enthusiasm. "Boy, if I owned a little number like that—!"

"It's really got power," said Vince, and the pair of them went off into a long rigmarole of technicalities and performance statistics. (I asked Charlie later whether Vince Haggarty knew his stuff on motorbikes, and Charlie shrugged and said he seemed to know as much as he, Charlie, knew, so it seems a great deal of bullshit-artistry was being indulged in by both parties.)

"You're the chap from Jim's Gym, aren't you?" Vince asked, as the technicalities tailed away.

"That's right."

"I was in there the other day. O'Connor's used to be my gym, in my competition days, but I knew Jim's quite well. Don't get around to much serious training any more, more's the pity. Have you got time for a drink?"

"I was just going to drop in somewhere myself."

So they went along to the Horse and Plough, a rural nest in deepest Dean Street, and Vince bought pints for himself and Charlie, and they sat in the corner furthest from the music and talked. Vince's approach was less than subtle.

"They cost money, bikes like that," he said.

"Don't I know it! But I'm saving up," said Charlie, playing the enthusiastic innocent (which he, by nature, most definitely was *not*). "And I'm getting the odd job, posing for ads and that, and I'm putting all that money aside. It's fun—great. I enjoy it."

"Really? I used to do a bit of posing when I was in competition shape. It was a bit extra, but I always thought the money was pretty poor."

"Yeah, it's not riches. But it's going to be great seeing myself when those ads come out!"

"I'm on the other side of the camera now," said Vince, casually lighting up a cigarette. "It pays better, and I've got to the age when it's just too much of a sweat to keep in shape."

"You're a photographer?" said Charlie, still with that boyish enthusiasm. "What sort of work do you do?"

"Oh, this and that," said Vince. "I could put work your way, if you were interested."

"Really?" said Charlie, as if he were auditioning for children's television.

"Depending on what you're willing to do."

"Oh, I'll do anything," said Charlie.

Vince took a sip of his drink.

"Watch it someone doesn't take you up on that," he said.

"Oh, I just meant I'd do posters, TV ads, posing, mod-elling—whatever's going."

Vince was looking at him hard across the table.

"I could put jobs your way where you could earn more than you'll ever get from that sort of work. Un-usual jobs . . ."

Charlie frowned, as if bewildered.

"What sort of thing?"

"Specialist work . . . Come on, you must have some idea of what I'm getting at. Now and again I do a bit of work for the sex mags, for example. I could use you on that. Depending on what you're willing to . . . show."

Charlie put on a particularly vacuous smile.

"I haven't got anything to hide," he said.

"That's what most people feel these days," said Vince. "Most modern people. Attitudes are healthier now than they were. And most of the magazines I work for are on sale perfectly openly—the police take a very permissive line these days. They know it's a kind of safety-valve. Now, just for instance, I could do a sequence of you for one of the gay mags—*Hom,* or *Fly.*"

"Isn't *Fly* the British Airways in-flight magazine?"

"No, it isn't. It really isn't. In *Fly* the fly is ever-open, if you get my meaning."

"Oh, I get your meaning."

"Would you be interested in that kind of work?"

Charlie made a great show of slow thinking.

"It's not something I've ever considered," he said at last.

"You've no moral objections?"

"Oh no. Still, we've always been a pretty religious family. I wouldn't want my old mum to see it."

"Hom and *Fly* are not magazines your old mum is likely to pick up casually."

"I wouldn't want my mates to see, either," said Charlie, going all teenager. "But I don't suppose they'd be likely to buy it."

"Of course, we'd go on to the other stuff, if that went well . . . Twosome stuff—know what I mean? Various combinations and possibilities."

"What about money?"

"Oh, you'd be well paid."

"How well paid?"

Charlie stuck to the point. If Vince had been brighter he would have seen that Charlie's financial acumen did not jell quite with the ingenuousness he had flaunted hitherto. I don't think Charlie had much faith in the special police fund he was supposed to get paid from. Anyway, Vince did not see the discrepancy, and in the end they came to an agreement for £75 for the first session. It wasn't riches, but Charlie thought that was about the sort of sum that someone inexperienced in that kind of thing might be willing to accept.

"Right," said Vince, when that part of the negotiations was concluded. "Well, here's to success! This could well be the beginning of a very nice little sideline for you."

"I hope so," said Charlie, smiling shyly. "When will we have the session?"

Vince got out a grubbly little diary-notebook, a habit he had perhaps acquired from Bob Cordle.

"What about Tuesday evening?"

"Fine. Where?"

"Hmmm. Haven't used my place for some time. Let's say there—52 Dedham Road, NW2—around six-thirty."

That was a big disappointment for Charlie, who had hoped to find out what locale had been hired to make up for the loss of the *Bodies* studio. But he smiled his enthusiastic amateur smile, and asked:

"Should I bring anything with me? Wear anything special?"

Vince drained his glass.

"What the guys who read those magazines are interested in, you'll have with you anyway." He got up, clapped Charlie on the shoulder, and said: "See you Tuesday."

"It was more of the old slave-market stuff," said Charlie, when he reported to me, eating a takeaway pizza at our flat.

"I told you you weren't going to enjoy it as much as you thought," I said.

"It's like being weighed by the pound in a meat-market."

"My wife is under the impression that it's only women who are regarded in that fat-livestock way," I said.

"I never said it was only women," said Jan. "Still, it does seem as if it's only *men* who buy flesh wholesale like that, doesn't it?"

I had to admit that was a clever hit. I sat there wondering whether it was true.

CHAPTER 15

When Charlie, on his lunch-hour a couple of days later, popped down to New Scotland Yard to tell me about the photographic session at Vince Haggarty's flat, I fetched Garry Joplin in, and Archie Nelson from the Dirty Squad. Most of the men in that squad are thick as two planks, and have to be told that the works of D. H. Lawrence, not to mention those of Oscar Wilde, are now generally available to the impressionable public, and that all sorts of things they were told in Sunday school were wrong are now legally indulged in around the Metropolitan area of London without the whole fabric of society falling apart. Archie Nelson was not thick and not corrupt, and he was the pleasantest and loneliest guy in the Dirty Squad, if somewhat irritating by reason of his world-weary air. When Charlie saw us all there he said he was embarrassed at having to tell his story to an audience, but he was not in the least embarrassed, or, I suspect, embarrassable.

In fact, Charlie had enjoyed himself disgracefully.

Vince had had an assistant with him in the Dedham Road flat—a thin, hollow-cheeked young man, with sharp, rat-like eyes. His name was Mick Spivey. He did a lot of shifting around of lights and equipment, but Charlie suspected from things he said that his place in the set-up was mainly organizational and financial. He had a wheedling manner and a whiney voice, and Charlie did not like him at all. When he got there Mick and Vince were shifting furniture around and putting the heavy lights on to frames, or suspending them from the ceiling. Charlie helped them for a bit, and Vince said that was all right because a muck sweat could be very attractive, and anyway could be wiped off. The props of the session were pretty simple: the sofa, one or two of the African wall-hangings, and so on. Then Charlie began taking off his clothes, and the session got under way.

Vince had got certain minimal items of clothing, for purposes of titillation, and the session began with Charlie in these. There were briefs, over which Charlie popped, a special pair of ragged Y-fronts out of which Charlie popped, and a jock-strap which he was required to play coyly with. Coyness, Vince and Mick decided after consultation in serious voices, didn't come easily to Charlie, so they gave that up. Then they photographed him without the clothing props, sitting astride the arm of the sofa, smouldering nakedly in front of the ethnic drapes, or lying invitingly on the rug by the fireplace. Then they went into the bathroom, which was in fact a shower room, and quite the smartest room in the flat, newly redecorated in white and blue tiles of a modernistic design.

"Very photogenic, showers," said Vince, as if Hitchcock had not made that discovery long before. Then they had had great fun with veils of water and splashes on the camera lens for some time, until Vince's girlfriend had arrived, shown herself at the door of the bathroom, and that had put an end to the session.

"Erections are not allowed," said Archie Nelson, in the pedantic manner of a local government officer reciting building regulations, "but otherwise there's nothing there that we would pounce on, so far as I can see. It all sounds very much within the guidelines we lay down."

"Yeah," said Charlie, rather miffed. "But that was to be expected, wasn't it? It was my first time."

"Any indications of anything more dubious lined up for the future?" I asked.

"Well, there's a session with leather gear arranged for some time next week."

The Dirty Squad man shrugged, with an air of Tiresias who has foresuffered all.

"They haven't given me a location yet," Charlie went on, "but I think it'll be in the new studio, for variety's sake. They said the readership of *Fly* and *Leather* overlapped. But then there was something else . . ."

"Yes?"

"Before I went they were tossing around various possible future projects. What they were talking about was films—what they called 'twosome films.' Me—with girls, other men, boys. They said the others would all be white."

"Why?" I asked, fascinated, as if Vince felt himself bound in some way by the Equal Opportunities law.

"I think he'd got the idea that I fancied his girlfriend. Well, he *knew* I fancied his girlfriend . . . But what he actually said was there was no great market for black on black. 'It doesn't appeal,' he said. 'Quite apart from the fact that it's damned difficult to film.' I can imagine the contrast does work better."

"What did you say to his proposals?"

"I expressed some doubt about the boys. I thought that would be in keeping with the character. As for the rest, I said I'd probably be willing."

Archie Nelson was still showing signs of lack of interest, so I said: "Was that all?"

Charlie screwed up his face.

"Not quite. This all took up the time while I was dressing. I was just about to leave, and Vince was handing over the money—in cash, and *very* welcome—when he said: 'There's more where that comes from, if you're willing.' And of course I said I was very willing. Then he said, sort of lightly, but watching me: 'We can fix you up with some real kinky jobs, if you have a mind to do them.' And I said, lightly too, that I thought I'd be ready for most things . . . And that was about it."

"Right," I said. "So we just wait until he gives out a few more details on what kind of kinky he has in mind."

Archie Nelson yawned, infuriatingly.

"We can't do much, even on the kinky stuff these days. About the worst we can do is report them to the RSPCA if there's animals involved. But keep your ears open so as to learn more about the distribution. There was this other bloke—what did you say his name was?"

"Mick Spivey," said Charlie. "A right ratty little guy. Sell his mother for a tuppence-off washing powder coupon."

"Keep close to him. Try and find out where their stuff is stored. There'll be films and videos, and they will take up a fair bit of space. Remember anything you hear about who the customers are, and how they get the stuff out to them."

"Right. So I'm to stay with it?"

"Yes," I said. "Until they really start pressing you to do something you wouldn't like."

"I don't pressure easily," said Charlie complacently.

"Remember the part you're playing," I said severely. "You're not you, you're him."

Charlie, I suspected, like most non-actors, found it difficult to keep up any other persona consistently.

The next time I heard from him it was by phone: he still had done nothing likely to raise the temperature of Archie Nelson even half a degree from its professionally reptilian cool. He had done the posing for the leather mag, but he said it was only "the same as before, only with cowhide." No shocks or surprises. The interesting thing from my point of view, though, was that the session had taken place in the new studio.

"Where was this?" I asked.

"That's the problem. I was told to go to Vince's pad, and we drove on from there. I didn't like to look around me too interested, like. It's the Elephant and Castle, that I do know. Perhaps two or three minutes from the Underground. It's an old warehouse, practically derelict, or at least bloody scruffy. There's some grubby old houses nearby, but a lot of them are empty, and there's a bit of ground with some of those houses they put up after the war."

"Prefabs?"

"That's right."

"Not many of those left. That should help us identify the place. It sounds a dump."

"It is, but they've done it up inside, of course. A hell of a lot of whitewash on the walls, and piles of drapes—a few ethnic ones from the girlfriend, some tartans and tweeds for the healthy outdoor feel, and lots of those pastel, satiny ones like poor old Wayne and that girl were posed against in those last pictures. Me and my leather were taken against pastel blue. I should think I looked great."

"You're getting a taste for this business."

"It's the cash they hand you in a brown envelope at the end of the sessions."

And Charlie rang off, obviously highly pleased with himself. He had certainly given me something to go on. I got straight on the phone to the Elephant station, and told them to give the relevant parts of Charlie's description to the boys on the beat and see what they made of it. In fact, two days later I was looking at a list of four possible locations sent me from the Elephant station when Charlie rang again.

"I want to see you."

"Proper see? Meal?"

"Yeah. I want to talk."

"Right. I've got to be here till two a.m. tonight, but I should be able to take an hour off early evening. What about six-thirty at the Knossos?"

We struck lucky at the Knossos. It was only just open,

and the atmosphere inside was funereal. Mr. Leonides, in fact, sported a black armband, and I supposed he had catered for a Greek funeral earlier in the day, and not a very jolly one either. The kitchen, however, did not seem to be affected, and the Dolmades that we began with were excellent. I stuck to lager because I was on duty, but Charlie insisted on a half-bottle of wine. We didn't talk until we were well settled into our food.

"What's happened?" I asked.

Charlie took a sip of his Bull's Blood.

"It was yesterday, when I finished work. Sometimes I go through the whole evening shift till nine—evening's our busy time, especially just after the working day finishes. More often, though, I finish at six, and one of the chaps takes over—one of the muscle boys wanting to earn a bit and train at the same time, or the boy you call the Anatomy Lesson. Well, last night I finished at nine, and I was just about to leave the office and lock up when I saw he was waiting for me in the corridor."

"Who? Vince?"

"No. Mick Spivey. I don't like this organization: it seems like the dirtier the job, the lower down the person who undertakes it. Todd Masterman delegates the dubious stuff to Vince Haggarty, and Haggarty delegates the practically untouchable stuff to Mick Spivey. Anyway, Mick looks the part to a T, and very out of place in a gym: barbel curls and cross-bench pullovers couldn't do much for *him*, I'm telling you. Anyway, he said he was pleased to see I was free—though he obviously knew I would be, and obviously knew the night I would be working late. I felt I had been watched. So he said would I care for a drink?"

"You're really getting out of the wholewheat and tomato juice circuit," I observed, watching him pour his second glass.

"I never was in it. So we went along to the Horse and Plough, strolling along in the dark, and we chatted as if there was no ulterior motive around in the world, and Mick asked me how I'd enjoyed the sessions so far, and I did my gushing schoolgirl act, about how great it was, and how I was looking forward to seeing myself in the mags, and what a great photographer Vince was, and how great he made me look, and I sickened myself, but that got us to the Horse and Plough, and the custom was fairly thin by then, because the theatres weren't out yet, and we found a table to ourselves. Mick insisted it was his treat, since he'd asked me along, and he got two pints, and later another two, and I let him, because I felt I'd earned that just by listening to his voice, which sounds like a pen nib scratching on glass. When we were halfway through the first pint, Mick said: 'I'm glad you're enjoying the sessions, because Vince thinks you're good. Says you've got talent. And I agree.' So I smiled a Cheshire cat smile, said 'Gee, thanks,' and waited."

"Then Mick said casually: 'We've got something coming up a bit out of the ordinary, if you're interested.' And I said: 'You know I'm always interested.' 'This one's for the fladge market,' Mick said, looking at me from under his eyelids, but real sharp. 'Lord, man, don't you ever make anything with straight sex?' I said, but laughing. 'Give me a break some time! You must have lots of dolls lining up to appear in a bit of good, old fashioned bedroom sex. Why not do some of that for a change?' "

"Good," I said, when Mr. Leonides, who had been fussing round the table as he brought our lamb, had gone. "You didn't jump straight into it. That's right. But do you think the character you're playing would have understood what the fladge market was?"

"We're pretty wised up in Brixton. And all sorts of things circulate there. I thought I shouldn't jump into it shouting 'Hooray! My life's ambition!' though."

"Oh no. Absolutely not."

"Anyway, then Mick started to explain. They'd been operating now as a going concern for five or six months, and as far as straight sex was concerned, they'd got a great little store of reels, with all the usual variations, and most of the obvious colour combinations. They were doing roaring business, especially in the video trade, and those films were going round and round like a fairground horse. Of course, he said, some of their early films were pretty amateur—"

"I can imagine," I said. "I've seen some of that kind of film."

"—so they'd need renewing eventually. Mind you, I think he was just saying that to keep me interested. I suspect most of their customers don't give a monkey's how amateur the thing is, provided they see what they paid to see. Anyway, the gist of the situation is that they're going all out after the other markets now."

"I can imagine," I said. "What role in this fladge epic does he have in mind for you? Will you inflict, or suffer?"

"Oh, inflict. I expect suffering would come under the heading of stereotyping—maybe get the film banned by the licensing board. So what he had in mind for me was an amusing little number, probably a fifteen- or twenty-minute job, he said, showing a birching. Me birching a white boy, or maybe two."

"I see," I said. "I wonder what Archie the Vice would say to that. Probably shrug his shoulders and say if that was all they couldn't touch Haggarty for it."

"Well, that's about what I did—shrugged my shoulders, and said I supposed I could do it, at least if they thought I would be convincing enough. Mick Spivey smiled and wheedled, and made me want to throw up at that. But that wasn't the end of it."

"No?"

"No. Mick leaned forward, all the time watching me with those sharp little eyes, and said: 'As to it being convincing, you don't need to worry about that. It'll be convincing all right. The trick is, you see, it'll be for real.' Well, that really got me, and I gawped at him quite genuinely. 'For real?' 'Yes—at least the first five or six strokes. More, if possible. The rest we fake, and re-use discarded shots from earlier strokes. That way what we show really carries authenticity—the twisted expressions on the boys' faces, the screams, the sweat. It can be very powerful.' Now that really got me. That did turn my stomach."

"I must say it doesn't do any good to mine," I said, pushing aside my plate.

"So I said: 'But who on earth can you get to do it? They must be nutters.' And he sat back in his chair, and smiled, and said: 'There's hundreds—thousands—of lads sleeping rough all over London. Girls too—we use them as well, quite a bit. They're desperate for money for food, often for drugs. The trick is knowing where to find them, because the police are always moving them on. I've got the trick. They know me. We use them in all sorts of films. Often they're only about fourteen or fifteen, and at that age you can make them look a lot younger. They're pretty desperate, you know—come from shocking homes, do anything for a square meal. We're a sort of charity, in a way. Like in this case, for example: we pay them for the appearance, then we pay extra for every stroke that's done for real.'"

"Oh my God," I said. "I love his charity."

"He really is a horrible guy," agreed Charlie, obviously murderously indignant. "I think all this really is sick. They get these poor bloody starving and bewildered kids, and then they do *that* to them."

"We certainly could get him on a charge for that, and that's some consolation. Pretty obviously they're also involving minors in straight sex films—we can get them for that too. How did the interview go from then on?"

"Well, I reacted normally, and I think that was right. It's not something anyone normal would like doing."

"Good. I expect yours was the usual reaction."

"Mick Spivey played down the nasty side. Said they wouldn't feel it next day, they were well paid—five pounds a stroke, it was riches to them, and so on. We went on discussing it for a bit, me making it clear I wasn't jumping over the moon about it, but gradually coming round. I said I was a bit uncertain, because after all there was acting involved, even if it was for real, and I wasn't an actor. Mick said I would do it fine, but if I wanted I could come and see another film of the same kind being made."

"Ah."

"He said that, the same evening he had in mind for filming me whopping these boys, there'd be another of the same kind done earlier on in the evening. They really turn them out wholesale, don't they? He said it wouldn't be the same, because this would be just pretend. The scenario they had, he said, was a man being whipped, and you just couldn't risk doing him an injury."

"Quite apart from the fact that grown men aren't likely to let themselves be whipped for five quid a pop."

"Exactly—though it was the industrial injuries side that he stressed. He said I could come along early to watch that, and it would give me some idea of the sort of *feeling* they wanted to get into the film."

"Christ—I can imagine what sort of feeling that would be."

"Finally I said I thought it probably would be all right —that I'd ring him before tomorrow if I changed my mind."

"When is this little job set up for?"

"Next Tuesday. So even if I don't do it, they've plenty of time to find a replacement."

"No," I said. "Say you'll do it. From our point of view it's practically an ideal set-up."

"I don't want—"

"No, of course you don't. What do you think I am? Say you'll do it, we'll have the joint cased, and the moment the thing starts being for real, we'll come in and take them."

Later that night, when I had an odd half-hour free, I drove over the river and down to the Elephant and Castle. Of the four addresses I had got from the local men, only one really matched up to Charlie's description. It was a two-storey warehouse near a little slum of prefabs, but well away from anything else. There were heavy curtains over such windows as there were on the second floor, but they could not hide the fact that there were lights on—very powerful lights, I thought. I parked the car two minutes away, and went up to the building. I walked around, and found at the side a door that led—I could see through a dirty window just beside it—to a flight of stairs. I felt the hinges, and they had had oil applied to them recently. As I stood there in the eerie darkness, with only the sound of the distant traffic to be heard, I realized that remotely, from inside the building, there were coming the sounds of people making love. What sex they were I was not quite sure, though I did suspect they were augmenting their cries, even hamming it up, for the sound-recording apparatus. But I heard enough to convince me that that night, too, Vince Haggarty was making one of his special contributions to British Film Year.

CHAPTER 16

I had a watch put on the building the moment I got back to the Yard, and I put the Elephant police on to making discreet inquiries into the ownership of the place. They found out that it had been empty since well before the current depression, and was let to Vince Haggarty for practically nothing. The firm's accountant was an enthusiast for "the sport," so presumably Vince had heard of the place through the old muscleboy network.

The watch reported that Vince remained a night-worker, even though the old imperative no longer remained. He was never seen around the building during the day, which made our preparations much easier. In one respect the loneliness and near-dereliction of the place suited us fine: there were any number of spots where I could hide men around the warehouse—and I had figured that I would use seven or eight to be on the safe side. On the other hand, there needed to be an observer there other than Charlie, whose evidence, as a participant, could be taken apart by a good defence lawyer. I needed to observe, too, in order to coordinate the men and choose the best moment for them to go in and stop the thing.

That proved rather less simple. I established (somewhat unorthodoxly, by going into the place) that the first floor was simply a large, high room, with no conceivable place to hide. There was a very large chest, but it was padlocked, and the lock of the padlock was oiled, so I figured it was likely to contain things needed during the filming. Most of the windows of the place were inconveniently high, but at the far end there was a lower one, over which the drape had been rather carelessly arranged, perhaps because most of the filming seemed to take place down the other end of the building, where the walls were hung with coloured materials. I walked around in the waste ground surrounding the place—which was a dump in every sense of the word—and picking through all the builders' waste, kids' discarded cans and glue bottles and general family effects, I found an ancient but substantial chest of drawers. I arranged to have it moved under the window after dark, and told the watching constable to make damned sure that none of the local scavengers took it.

Charlie kept me posted about arrangements, and on the Tuesday that was scheduled for the filming he phoned in the morning to say that he was leaving work early so as to be at Vince's Dedham Road flat at four o'clock. That should mean they would get to the Elephant by four-thirty, by which time it would be all but dark. The boys, Charlie said, were going to be fetched later, when the first piece of quickie-porn was in the bag. Charlie's adrenalin was running at the prospect of an exciting evening, but he repeated over and over that he wanted the thing stopped before it became serious. I assured him that he couldn't want it more than I did, and told him I'd be watching so as to pick the best moment.

I took Joplin with me to the Elephant, and six other sergeants and constables. Joplin's job was to marshall the forces, mine to give the signals. We left the detailed deployment till after the party began, though Garry had selected most of the positions: one was in the undergrowth of what had once been one of the prefab's vegetable patches, one was in the area steps of one of the derelict houses, the rest were in the cat-infested wastelands around the warehouse. I was at the back, waiting to climb on to my chest of drawers.

The film team arrived about four-thirty. Vince pulled up some way from the only streetlamp in the vicinity that was working, and he, Mick, Charlie, and an unknown bloke quickly and efficiently transferred the equipment into the warehouse, watched by the Portuguese girlfriend. The cameras they took home, apparently, after each session: the rests and tripods and frames and other less valuable impedimenta they left there, as I had ascertained during my illicit tour of the place. We gave them a few minutes to settle down, and to remember anything they might have left in the car, but it was an efficiently run operation, and nobody came out. So Garry, quietly, with nothing but signs, began deploying his men around the place. I had perhaps brought rather more than I needed, granted that the warehouse had only two exits, one of them apparently disused and rusted into unopenability. But I knew that Vince was (in appearance, at any rate) a physically capable man, I didn't know who else would be there, and I wanted to be safe rather than sorry.

When all the men were deployed, I thought it was time to take up my watch position. I clambered silently on to the chest, and looked through into the brilliantly lighted room. It was a chaos of cameras, tripods and lights, but one that was rapidly reducing itself to order. Vince was either a good general, or the films he shot were pretty simple to stage. Charlie, Mick and the other man were humping stuff around, and it was only a matter of minutes before things were in position to Vince's satisfaction. The Portuguese girlfriend took no part in this buzz of activity. She stood by the door at the far end from me, splendid in fur coat and caftan, coolly gazing at the scene as if it were nothing to do with her. Vince was shouting directions to the rest (the window was very ill-fitting, so I could hear talk, if it was not too low), but he never shouted any to her. If he had, of course, it is unlikely she would have understood.

By about five, all was apparently ready. The place was heated by a couple of oil heaters, placed by the area they were filming in, which was at the draped end furthest from me. Well rugged-up outside, I began to feel sorry for them inside, if they were going to take off their clothes. And of course they *were* going to take off their clothes. It wouldn't be that kind of film if they didn't.

Charlie was all right for the moment, lounging against a wall in a dark blue track-suit, and occasionally coming to warm his hands against a heater. Vince, too, had a heavy tweed sports jacket on, and a woollen scarf. But the other two, I thought, were going to earn their money.

It soon became clear how. Vince and Charlie brought over one of the heavy wooden frames usually used to fix lights to, and they placed it in the centre of the field of light.

"Right," said Vince. "Let's go. Take your clothes off, Harold. I think a loincloth would be appropriate, don't you?"

Harold was a fair-haired, willowy young man, very much a contrast to the run of bodies I'd been seeing in the course of this case. He took his clothes off, piled them up neatly in a corner, donned the ready-made loincloth that Vince handed him, and stood there shivering and banging his arms across his chest over by the heater. He did not even look at himself in the mirror that stood over by the door.

"Come on, come on," said Vince impatiently. "We've got to get this in the can before we fetch the boys."

He was standing by the frame holding two lengths of rope. Harold went over, raised his hands up to the cross-bar of the frame, and let himself be tied roughly in a spread-eagled position.

"Right," said Vince, surveying his inspired piece of improvisation. "Let's get a few shots of you before the action starts . . . Look terrified . . . Terrified, not tearful . . . Come on, for Chrissake—*fear!* . . . Oh well, that'll do, I suppose. I thought you called yourself an actor. You'd never get a job on *Mutiny on the Bounty*

. . . Right, my darling: take your clothes off, as only you know how."

He gestured the act of undressing to his girlfriend, who was standing over by the other heater. In a queenly, almost contemptuous manner she complied. She slid off the fur coat, and let it lie on the dusty floor, pulled the caftan over her head, and then took off such Western underwear as she had on. Then she stood there, leant slightly backwards, surveying them, her lips turned slightly downwards in an expression of distaste. She was the most stunning sight I had seen in years—the only fine body I had seen in this case that did not have the stain of anonymity upon it, that feeling of mass production. She was square-shouldered, to go with her height, and her breasts were large but firm, and every part of her expressed power and force.

"Very nice," said Mick Spivey, looking like a dwarf in her vicinity. "Very nice indeed."

Vince had gone to the chest over by the far wall, and taken out a long, shiny hide whip. Standard equipment, apparently. He handed it to her, and the corners of her mouth came up, slightly, into an expression of satisfaction. Perhaps she had fantasies of turning it on him. She stood there, magnificent, cracking the whip in the air experimentally a few times.

"Don't let her touch me with that," said Harold from his frame. "My skin is very sensitive."

"It won't come near you, Harold," muttered Vince impatiently.

And certainly he was as good as his word. It is difficult to convey the risible yet tacky nature of the filming that followed. First the girlfriend, looking splendid and fearsome, if only Vince's directorial skills could have cap-

tured it, was taken inflicting terrible punishment on the
vacant air. Then shots were taken of her standing before the frame, brandishing the whip threateningly at
Harold's back. Then came shots of the whip draped
across the shoulders of Harold, with Vince painting in
wealts with lipstick across his body between each shot.
Harold was shivering, quite genuinely. Cold had its uses
in a film of this kind, I decided, though I couldn't see its
helping much in the straighter sex productions. Vince
seemed less satisfied however, with the front shots he
took of Harold looking agonized, screaming with pain,
and begging for mercy. Actors' Equity are always giving fearful statistics of the numbers of their members
who are out of work, but one always suspects that a
great many of them richly deserve to be. Watching Harold trying to render simple emotions only confirmed
that belief. Finally Vince shook his head and gave up,
getting his own back by forgetting to untie Harold and
ignoring his pleas to be allowed down from his frame.
Finally he took a bit more film of the girlfriend brandishing her whip, sound-recorded the whip being
cracked against the warehouse wall, and then decided
that his latest fladge masterpiece was in the can, and
could be satisfactorily put together in the cutting-room.

Charlie, I could see, found all this intensely amusing.
If anyone chanced to look his way he was observing
things with an absorbed interest, but at other moments
his whole body was shaking with laughter. I too, on my
perch outside in the dank November weather, would
quite often like to have let out a roar of mirth. But it
wasn't *only* funny: the shoddy, improvised nature of it
was highly chuckle-inducing, it was true—the lights,
frame Harold was tied to, the lipstick weals. But then

there was that splendid naked body, all that beauty and force, which was lending itself to this tacky little piece of fantasy-fodder. It presented an inescapable contrast between the beauty of some bodies, and the ugly things that were done to them. Ah well—as I said to Garry earlier, I should restrain my tendency to moralizing monologues.

Now that this piece was done, to be spliced together at some future date to provide a highly unconvincing little thrill for the video viewers, they could start thinking about the next one. One could see why they did better with the real thing: Vince obviously had no talent at all for faking. Charlie now took pity and went and untied Harold, who quickly donned his clothes, muttering bitterly to himself. Why he kept his complaints to himself was obvious when he was kitted out again: he went to Vince to demand his payment, and Vince with obvious reluctance that was meant to imply dissatisfaction with his performance counted out a number of tens. The girlfriend had put on her clothes again with silent, consummate grace, her face expressing no emotion whatsoever. She was sailing towards the door as Vince paid off Harold, and he called her:

"Hey! Black cow!" She turned. He pointed to Mick. "You want lift? Drive?"

He mimed driving. She stood, impassively waiting, as Vince gave the car keys to Mick. I made to Garry Joplin one of our prearranged signs, the one meaning "Keep very low. Someone coming out." Mick tossed the keys up in his hand, asked Harold if he wanted a lift back over the river, and then the three of them came out, picked their way through the darkness to the car, and drove off.

Charlie and Vince were now getting down to work. After some thought Vince decided to shoot this lot of film down my end of the room, away from the drapes.

"The drapes are wrong," he said, showing his first faint glimmer of an artistic sense. "Down here is better —sort of bare, and hard. Like a peni—peni . . . Sort of prison. You know."

Charlie nodded, though I knew he was itching to supply the word himself. In a matter of minutes they had moved the lights and the cameras down, and positioned them to Vince's satisfaction. Then Vince went to the large box again, the one containing the props of his trade, and came up with two largish wooden frames, designed to be laid on the floor, with leather, buckled bracelets at either end. Charlie helped him hump them over, but it was Vince who positioned them in the pool of light, and then stood there contemplating them deeply, as if weighty questions of aesthetics were involved. Then he checked each camera meticulously.

"You've got to be dead careful you haven't done anything daft," he explained to Charlie. "With this sort of caper, there aren't any re-takes."

"Yeah, I can see that," said Charlie. "What exactly is it you want me to do?"

"Simple. Piece of cake. When they get here, I want it all to go very fast, see? At least until they're strapped down. I'll size 'em up, and if they look as if they might do it all right, I'll tell them to take their clothes off in the light, with the cameras rolling. As soon as they've done that, you take them and put them down on the frames —heads *there*, feet *there*, and you strap up their hands and their feet so the little buggers can't change their minds and walk out halfway. I won't get the birch out till they've got their clothes off—don't want to scare the little darlings too soon. Not that it *looks* so bad. You might walk forward carrying it—might get a good expression shot out of them. When you've tied 'em up, get hold of the birch again, then stand about . . . *here*, and when I tell you to, whop the one on this frame with all your might. Make it impressive, slow—sort of ritual, know what I mean? We'll have plenty of time between strokes, so we've got masses of film to play around with afterwards, and we'll film the other boy, waiting for his, and watching. Now—how shall we have you?" He looked at Charlie with the eye of a Hockney. "I think football shorts, don't you? Sort of gives the idea of school, don't you think? I've got several pairs here . . ."

"I've got shorts *on,*" said Charlie. "I thought this might turn out to be a schoolboy caper."

Charlie really went too far. He was meant to be amiably dim. He was more in character when he refused to strip off and get all goosepimply waiting for the boys to arrive.

"OK, OK. Well, look, you just stand over there in the shadows, down by the door, and you come out stripped when I've got them in the light there. That's when I'll hope for some expression shots. The birch is over there in the props box . . . Was that a car?"

It had indeed been a car. I had gestured to have the men lie very low, and it drew up in the same position it had occupied before. Three shadowy shapes got out, and one of them ushered the other two towards the warehouse. I didn't get more than a glimpse of them until they came upstairs and into the light. I guessed they were both about fifteen or sixteen, though they looked younger. Both were scruffy, and probably dirty, and neither looked as if he was getting regular food. The sturdier of the two had a certain aggressive cockiness about him, suggesting he could make out on his own. The other was a pathetic figure—pale, withdrawn, and almost certainly on drugs. He walked into the bright lights of the warehouse studio, dazed, as if he scarcely knew where he was or what he was doing there.

"Come over here," called Vince, and they came over to the bright lake of light down my end of the room. Vince gestured Mick towards the cameras.

"Right—take off your clothes," he said, when they had come into the shooting space.

"Here, wait a minute, Mister" said the more wide-awake of the two. "Before we do anything we want the money."

"After. You get paid afterwards."

"No, we don't. That's not on. We agreed between us, Colin and me: money first or no deal. Money for being in it in the first place, and then for six strokes. Then we get extra afterwards if we agree to more. That's fair. We don't do a thing until we get the cash in our pockets."

Cursing, Vince took his wallet out of his inside pocket and counted out a number of notes for each of the boys. The aggressive one counted his and tucked them into a back pocket, then he counted out his friend's, and put his away likewise. The friend was withdrawn into some kind of inward contemplation.

"Right. Now take your clothes off," said Vince, nodding again to Mick, who set the cameras rolling and concentrated them on the more with-it one of the pair, since the other was stripping off his clothes as if in a dream. It was when they were nearly naked that Charlie came forward, looking genuinely threatening, carrying the birch. I could just see the boys' faces: the cockier boy was startled, but put on immediately an expression of bravado; the other boy's eyes suddenly focused themselves on Charlie, registered a sudden understanding of what was to happen to him, and then changed to terror and panic. Mick Spivey's camera, of course, was on the wrong boy—a typical example of Vince's incompetence.

As Charlie seized the terrified boy and began strapping him on to the frame, I made the second of my signs to Garry Joplin: the men were to come forward and collect around the door to the warehouse.

The boy's hands were now buckled to the frame, but he was lashing out with his feet. Charlie took them in both hands, and then knelt on one, and buckled the other into the straps. Then he seized the other leg, and the boy was helpless. His body was feebly thrashing around in the limits of its mobility. Vince, behind the cameras, was rubbing his hands with satisfaction.

"This'll look marvellous," he said.

The other boy's air of bravado was wearing thin.

"This'd better be worth it," he said obscurely, as Charlie took him and stretched him across the frame. I had a glimpse round the side of the warehouse of shadowy figures gathering round the door. As Charlie stood up, took up his birch and began flourishing it with experimental strokes in the air, I gave him a few seconds, to make sure they were ready, and then I gave Joplin the third sign.

Then we went in and took them.

CHAPTER 17

A policeman develops antennae that twitch in the company of a born sneak. I don't think I needed those, though, to guess where the weak link was going to be found in those four people we took back to the Yard. I set Garry Joplin on to talk to the two boys, to get evidence of the offer they'd been made, of any work they'd done for Vince before; Vince Haggarty himself I left to cool his heels in a waiting-room; I talked to Mick Spivey. Charlie had said he would shop his own mother for a soap coupon, and he was dead right. Ratty in appearance, and rat by nature—that about sums up Mick Spivey. I had no sooner offered the usual inducements to cooperation than he was spilling the beans in an eager and ingratiating manner that quite turned the stomach.

Vince Haggarty, I learned, had slid into the porn video branch of his new profession almost as soon as he had mastered the elementary techniques of filming. Whether this was because he knew he had not enough talent ever to rise very high in the more legitimate side of the business, or from an inborn tendency to gravitate towards the grubby Mick didn't speculate. He, Mick, had come into the business as soon as it had begun to get off the ground—he had no particular title in the organization, but he acted as business manager, organizer of distribution, and general odd-job man. Oh, and— though he did not mention this himself—principal recruiter for all the more dicey films. The set-up had a list of customers that was growing all the time, and the quickie films to satisfy this market had to be turned out with equal speed. Be they ever so shoddily made, apparently, the new titles were snapped up by the mail-order customers as soon as they were put in the catalogue.

"And where were these videos kept?" I asked.

"Oh, in Todd Masterman's second garage. You'll find a catalogue and a list of subscribers there too. Sometimes we sell copies outright, we have a number of cinemas that take our stuff, but mostly we circulate them to private customers for a whacking fee. Todd didn't want them stored at his place, naturally—"

"Naturally," I said. "Mr. Clean, and all."

"—right. But there was no room at Vince or my places, and the rent he charges for the garage makes it worth his risk. Or so he thought. He always imagined that his reputation in the business would keep him clear of all this."

"He's going to find that he was wrong. That's not the sum total of his interest in this, is it?"

"Oh no. He put up money for cameras and equipment in the beginning, and that brought him a quarter share. Then, any time he put us on to anybody—people on his books, for example—we paid him a quarter of anything we paid them. It was a nice little sideline for him because the agency isn't all that flourishing. It was a good idea, but it was just a bit too specialized ever to take off in a big way."

So that was it. I talked to Vince, of course, and we fetched in the films and catalogues and the subscribers list from Todd Masterman's Wimbledon home. Pretty soon we took in Todd himself as well, and before long we had the porn film business sewn up. Garry got a lot more detail out of the only one of the boys he could really talk to. The sleeping-rough kids form a little—or not so little, these days—confraternity. Mick had quite a following, both of boys and girls, because he was often among them offering them jobs which, however grubby or nasty, were acceptable because of the pressures of hunger or the need for drugs. And some, I suppose, enjoyed it, for I must not sentimentalize them. Anyway, Mick was almost popular with them, though only as a source of food, drugs or excitement.

They were a sad pair, those boys. Garry did a good job with them, being much nearer their age than I was, and a much warmer person, but the only one he could help was the one who needed it least. He contacted his parents, patched things up, sent them off together. Probably the lad would have gone home eventually anyway. Equally probably he'd take off again at some time.

The other boy had been placed in care by his mother when he was two. He'd had a succession of foster homes, had run away at fourteen from an institution. We had to return him to one, but it was obvious it wouldn't last. Even before he had run away the first time he was on the road to being an addict. Now he was hopelessly far along that road. He needed the sort of constant and intensive care and support that nobody seems willing to pay for. Garry said he would be dead before he was twenty, and I knew he was right.

We both of us conveniently forgot the money that had been handed to the pair by Vince in the warehouse studio. I couldn't see Vince asking for it back.

I got varying stories and varying emphases about their own personal roles in the business from Mick and Vince and Todd Masterman, but in one thing they were unanimous: they knew nothing about the *Bodies* murders. Why connect them with that? They had not intended filming that night, had not been in the Windlesham Street area at the time, knew nothing whatsoever about the business. One thing they were quite sure about was that it was nothing to do with them.

And I was equally sure it was.

I'd seen the contents of Masterman's garage when they had been brought in. Now I took Joplin and we inspected them in detail. Much of the stuff was duplicate video tapes to be sent round to subscribers. Apart from those, there was the master copy of each film, a master catalogue with printed versions for the subscribers, and a list of those subscribers themselves—or

"members," as they were called, of the Speciality Video
Club.

That members list was fascinating. I found that several of the names rang a bell. There was that clergyman
in the West Country who had written to Phil Fennilow
offering to finance a film of *Lesbia Brandon.* There
were names of people who I was pretty sure were MPs,
though none of them gave the House of Commons as
their address, and most of them apparently lived on
farms—engaged in tax-deduction agriculture, no doubt.
And unless I was much mistaken there were at least two
members of the Metropolitan CID.

The things that interested Garry and me were the
films and the catalogue of the films. Well, naturally, you
will say: policemen are known to have sewer minds and
childish tastes. Actually I'd seen more than enough of
such products in my time to last me out, and even
Garry, after the first incredulous chortles were over,
said they really were a terrible drag. You have to have a
certain stamina to enjoy a concentrated diet of that
stuff.

And a concentrated diet was what we had to take. You
don't want to hear about it, do you? If you go in for that
kind of viewing, you'll know the sort of thing we had to
watch; and if you don't you can let your mind range in
smutty speculation. There were men and women doing
perfectly ordinary everyday things, but also things
more outré or acrobatic. There were men and men,
women and women, men and boys, women and boys,
men and girls, girls and Alsatians; there were rubber
films, leather films, whip films, bondage films—well, you
name it, they catered for it. They had—you had to hand
it to them—been awfully quick in getting their cata-

logue together. The originals were all nicely divided up into the various kinks, and the titles gave away the essential facts about their contents: *Buddy Pals; She plus She; Youth in Bloom; Little Girl,* and so on. The card index gave us the dates on which they were filmed, showing that, until recently, Vince had made use of every evening when the *Bodies* studio was hired out to Bob Cordle—this meant most of them were filmed on a Monday or a Wednesday. More recently things had become more flexible with the hiring of the new studio.

We took the straight sex ones first, running through them until we had got a clear impression of the various "actors" involved, then speeding them up to get a rough idea of whether there was anything of interest in the rest of the film, other than the basic biological interest. They were a lot more entertaining speeded up. I recognized Susan Platt-Morrison in one film—a most professional performance: she looked like a very high-class whore laid on for some visiting Sheik. I also recognized Vince's black girlfriend, and some of the faces I had seen when flicking through *Bodies* magazine, but otherwise found nothing of interest.

When we started in on the more out-of-the-way material, we both recognized someone at once.

"That's—oh my God, that's the lad I've been interviewing," said Garry Joplin.

It was the more confident of the two boys, being introduced to sex by a buxom and all-too-confident lady.

"Ugh," I said.

"That's really sick," said Garry.

"Still," I said thoughtfully, "put it into *Der Rosenkavalier* and everybody says 'Ooh, isn't it gorgeous?' "

"Der Whatsit?"

"An opera by Richard Strauss. You can cover a multi-tude of sins with heavy orchestration."

And so it went on. We saw Susan Platt-Morrison again in the Lesbian ones, and the Portuguese girlfriend seemed to have made a speciality of S-M material, which perhaps, if you had Vince Haggarty as a boy-friend, you might feel inclined to. Various sad-looking waifs of both sexes kept popping up in the films, submit-ting to being spanked or seduced by various confident adults of both sexes. After a while the same faces, usu-ally giving the same half-hearted performances, be-came monotonous.

"I say, I've just had a thought," I said eventually. "I haven't seen Denny Crabtree."

"You will. Plenty of time."

"No, but he said he was in a straight sex job. We've seen all those."

"He also said you didn't see his face, didn't he?"

"Yes. But there weren't any like that . . . Anyway, keep it rolling."

It was three or four films later (the films ran, on aver-age, about ten or fifteen minutes, by the way, but we mostly saw them in a much shorter time by speeding up) that I called out to Garry:

"Stop . . . Can you show that one again from the beginning?"

"It's only just started anyway," said Garry, rewinding.

"I know . . . It's just that . . ." The film started again, with a long, lingering shot of a heavily muscled back. "That's Crabtree, I'm sure of it."

"How can you be sure? These musclemen all look alike."

And I really didn't know how I knew. As Garry said,

one of the things that had struck me, browsing through the magazines, and again at the contest in Aberdeen, was the essential *sameness* of the bodies: take a photomontage of the line-up for Mr. Universe or whatever, and block out the faces, and there you were with essentially the same body, over and over. Or with all the white ones alike and all the black ones alike. But Crabtree's was the body that I had seen most in close-up, and for quite a long period of time. I knew intimately his double biceps pose, and his back lat spread pose. But perhaps what actually made me sure that this was Crabtree was a certain awkwardness in the filming, with the camera concentrating obstinately on the back and shoulders, and cutting off consistently at the neck.

"That's him. I'd swear it," I said. "Though I'm not sure how we'd ever prove it. What did you say this one was called?"

"Naughty Girlie."

"Oh dear . . . Oh Denny . . . You'd better carry on, Garry."

The film proceeded on its inept way. The camera backed away from the magnificent shoulder that made up its foreground shot, and there came into focus, facing Denny, a child in a cotton shift. A girl of—what?—ten, eleven in looks, yet perhaps older in fact. Slowly, inexpertly, yet with a childish parody of adult seductiveness that she must have seen in films, she slowly took off the shift, then took off her socks and shoes, then began to remove her underwear.

"That's enough." I said to Garry, and he stopped the projector. "Switch on the light." When I had blinked in the sudden access of light I turned to Garry, and saw that he was thinking the same thing as I.

"Have you got the card index catalogue there, Garry?"

"Yes."

"What date was this one filmed?"

"Let's see . . . November the seventh."

"The seventh. Exactly one week before the murders. . . . You saw who it was didn't you?"

"I think so."

"I just had the vague feeling at first, and couldn't really place her. I thought it might have been in connection with some other case."

"It wasn't in connection with any case," said Garry.

I put my head in my hands.

"No. It was poor old Leonides's daughter."

It was twenty to three when we arrived yet once more at the Knossos. Mr. Leonides, portly and sweating from a busy lunch-hour, bustled forward waving a menu.

"Good afternoon, gentlemen. Will it be three?"

"Not exactly. We won't be eating." The last little knot of lunchers began to gather their things together at a table by the door. "You'll be locking up now, will you?"

"Yes. I should have done it at half past."

"Then come and sit with us, will you?"

Mr. Leonides bustled the last of the eaters out, cheerily farewelling them, and perhaps it was my imagination that thought it detected signs of strain behind the cheeriness.

"There *is* just time for a little drink," he said hopefully when he returned, "if you gentlemen—"

"No. No drink," I said. "Would you sit down, Mr. Leonides? I'm afraid I don't know any way of making this conversation pleasant, and I'm sad because I've known you for a long time. I've got to talk with you in connection with the *Bodies* murders. It's about your daughter. . . ."

There was a long silence. Mr. Leonides had sat down, and he gazed for a long time at the red and white check of the tablecloth, without speaking.

"You mustn't blame her too much," he said finally, looking up at us. "She is not a bad girl. Silly. Young for her age. Not realizing. But not bad."

"Your daughter isn't the one to blame," I said. "I want to know exactly how it happened. Is she at home?"

"No, at school. I tell you about it. I tell you exactly how it happened. Though I didn't hear till much later, you understand. Like I say, she's a good girl. Very hard-working, willing. Maybe I keep her a little close—you understand? I not want her to be like some of these English girls—talking about contraceptives when they only ten, eleven. Is not nice. Is not the Greek way."

"It's not very often the English way," protested Garry.

"Too often. I not like. So I send her to very nice school. Private. The Dorothea Beale School, in Highgate. Very good standard—you know. Well—that's fine: she very happy. *Only*—only all the other girls, they come from families much richer than her—you understand? You know how children feel about that? Their fathers are men in the City, Harley Street, the House of Commons. And the restaurant trade? Well, when there's a depression it hits us first. Hard. Business lunches—yes, still plenty of those. Private people, couples, families—trade *way down*. We scrape to make a living, scrape to send her to that school. We do not have anything over for luxuries."

"And she found she couldn't keep up with the other girls?"

"Just in little things, first. She worry. They have, she not."

"How old is she, by the way?"

"Thirteen. She go to this school a year and a bit. So you see, she come up to her second Christmas there. And the big event of the year at the school—it is the Christmas party. Very posh and elegant, and all the young ladies allowed to invite a young man. And all the girls have very fine dresses—new one each year. Point of honour, you understand? Can't wear the same one as last year. My Elena she say she alter, no one know, but my Maria say *everyone* know, and she'd be shamed, and Nikos would be there, and see it, and so it went on."

"Nikos?"

Mr. Leonides looked up at me, a sharp expression in his eye.

"Yes—you see, she have a boyfriend to take. Was not serious, you understand—or was not *decided*. But was serious, and we hope. They are too young to know, but his father hope, I hope. His father my oldest friend in England. He have been here much longer. He come here thirty years ago, and more, after the Civil War in Greece. Nikos, Nick he call himself, is youngest child. I come fifteen, seventeen years ago. Maria is our only, two years younger than Nikos, but we hope."

"And they?"

"They?" Mr. Leonides expanded his hands in a generous gesture. "They loved. You think that is not possible at that age?"

"No. I didn't say that."

"Is possible. Is true. They love like Romeo and Juliet,

and we say: 'Soon—in five years' time—then maybe
. . .' " He sighed. "So don't say we was pushing them
into it, because we wasn't. Just talking, and saying
maybe. In other ways Maria think I'm terrible hard
father, but not for that."

"And are you strict?"

"Yes. Sure, I'm strict. It's right to be strict in a world
like we have it now. I want her where I can see her, or
where I know what she's doing. Is that wrong? I don't
want her out everywhere, meeting all sorts of people I
don't approve of. What happened proved me right."

"Who did she meet?" asked Garry.

Leonides paused, and resumed his staring at the tablecloth. At last he said:

"There's a café—two doors down, opposite the *Bodies*
place. She used to go there, drink coffee, play the machine there. I thought—two doors away, can't come to
no harm. Like the fool I was! She meet there with some
kids—rough kids, kids with no home, sleeping under
the bridges, in railway stations, doorways, anywhere.
They're in there, drinking coffee too, and playing the
machines. Because they're doing work for this photographer—what's his name?"

"Vince Haggarty."

"Is him. And he pays them good money, and they do
dirty things in front of a camera. Is pretty, pleasant, yes?
But you know all about this. When they get their
money, they come out and buy food at the café, hang
around, and that's how Maria meet them and talk to
them. And she hears about the money, and she thinks
about the dress she wants, and she starts saying at home
here that perhaps she can pick up something in the
Oxfam shop, or on the stall in the East End, and her

mother says, 'Fine, if you can find something that you want and it don't cost much.' But in fact she waits for this Haggarty to come into the café, and one night he does, to talk to one of these kids, and he sees Maria, and I don't know how it happen, but he make her an offer. And she say yes."

He put his face in his hands.

"She didn't understand," I suggested.

"Of course she didn't understand!" he exploded. "Not one little bit. He say she go there, take off her clothes, maybe play around a bit. Of course she not understand. But one night she go, and she is gone two, three hours, and when she come back I say 'You stop hanging around in that damned café all evening.' God help me—if I'd known what she'd been doing!"

"When did you find out?"

"Not for a time. She is very quiet after that. Sometimes breaks out into tears, and when we ask what the matter is, she say, 'Nothing.' We think it is her age. But it get worse, not better. She start getting hysterical, wouldn't tell us nothing, never went to the café, never went out nowhere. Then one day, suddenly, out it all comes."

"A week later?" I suggested. "A week after the filming?"

He thought a lot, before replying:

"Yes. Suddenly her mother ask her for the hundredth time, 'What's the matter?' and this time she answers: she bursts out sobbing and starts to tell . . . I am off-duty in the restaurant. I listen to her . . . I don't want to tell you what she told us."

"It's not necessary," I said gently. "I think we know about as much as we need."

"But she told us in the kitchen through there, and we sat and listened, and we not realize that Nikos come in."

"Her boyfriend?"

"Yes. He is like family. He come in back door, always he is like my own son. His father, my friend Stavros, he have Greek restaurant in Dean Street, so Nikos is always backward and forward for something or other. And he stand there, and he listen, and we don't know he's there till he rush out and slam the door."

"What did he do?"

Leonides looked at me, and did not answer for some time.

"I think you know."

"How did he get the gun?"

"He? Gun? His father, he is old Civil War man. Escape to Albania, not like it there, gets away to Jugoslavia, then to England. He is a man of many guns, many enemies. He teach his son—is *necessary* to shoot, he says."

"And then he came back and—?"

"Yes. One after the other. Not thinking, not caring . . ."

Leonides's eyes were dark with the pain of it. I thought. There had been something about the killings —the wholesale nature of it, perhaps—that had seemed to mark it out as the work of a madman. But perhaps what it really was was the work of an adolescent. I remembered the small footprint in the dust of the staircase.

Most of the rest of it I'd worked out before. Wayne Flushing had been such a poor poser that Bob Cordle's session had gone on much longer than usual. Wednesday night was Vince Haggarty's night, and perhaps he was sitting around somewhere in Windlesham Street, waiting for Bob to turn the lights out and go home. But someone—someone whom Haggarty had used, or, more likely, someone close to someone Haggarty had used, someone who had never seen him—had not known that his session that night was delayed. He had run up the stairs, listened to the session in progress, then dashed up to the doorway and let fly. There were photographers, there were nearly naked models. They must be the people he wanted to get. It was mad, wholesale revenge. Perhaps it was the all-or-nothing mentality of a fifteen-year-old?

"Why are you telling me this?" I asked. "The son of your oldest friend . . ."

"Of course I would not tell you it if he was living," said Mr. Leonides. I started. The confusion of his tenses, with present often serving for past, had not prepared me for that.

"He could not live with what he had done," he went on. "Not when he found out who he had killed, someone who had nothing to do with . . . with my Maria. Four people who had nothing to do with it at all. He shot himself. His father tell the coroner it is the O-levels which he do next year. Is much pressure on young people with exams these days, with so much unemployment. The coroner accept that is the reason. We bury him one day—it was a day you come here yourself . . . It was a funeral party you saw. His father, he never be the same, I think."

What started as a massacre seemed to be ending as a pathetic little story. Perhaps it was going to be one of those cases that we silently call closed.

"I must talk to your daughter," I said.

"Do you must? Is better now. She go back to school. She begin to forget. Why you need talk to her? You see that damned film. You hear from me all she told us. Is enough, more than enough. Why you have to go and get her to stir up in her mind all those horrible memories?"

"I'm afraid I have to hear about it in her own words," I said, collecting my papers together and not looking at him, because talking to his daughter was not something I wanted to do at all.

"Then I come," announced Mr. Leonides, standing up. "I come see you don't upset her. You not bully her. I know you police. You not nice with young girls."

He was becoming too obstructive. He was beginning to annoy me.

"Don't be a fool. You know me. Of course we will be gentle with her."

"No. I not trust you. I come to protect my little girl."

"That's not possible, Mr. Leonides."

"Of course I come. A father with his little daughter? Why is not possible?"

I looked down at the floor, at the pinstripe trousers holding up the substantial body, and at the little feet in patent leather shoes—shoes not more, I felt sure, than six and a half, or seven.

"Because you're still part of the case, Mr. Leonides," I said.

CHAPTER 18

Like so many stories I had been told in the course of the *Bodies* investigation, Mr. Leonides's proved to be true up to a point. What it was that made me dissatisfied with it I'm not quite sure, but I think it was the way everything tied up so neatly.

Talking to the man's daughter, though, was going to be a bit of a problem—and not just because it was likely to prove both difficult and distasteful. Certainly I couldn't have either of the parents sitting in, so according to Judges' Rules I had to have someone *in loco parentis.* On an inspiration I rang from the Knossos to the headmistress of the Dorothea Beale School, and learned that Maria would not yet have left. I asked her if she would set aside a room for us and sit in on the interview, and when she agreed I drove to New Scotland Yard and collected a WPC. I left Garry Joplin with the two Leonideses at the Knossos. He told me later that when the restaurant opened for business at six-thirty, Leonides's geniality was for once discernibly forced.

The headmistress had sounded a sensible woman, and proved to be so. Whether or not, like the original Miss Beale, she was impervious to Cupid's darts I could not know, but she seemed unlikely to be surprised by the nastier sides to the present-day love industry. She sat beside Maria, now and again at moments of stress taking her hand, but otherwise giving me a fairly free hand. I had told her that I had to get at the truth now, otherwise the pressure of lies and evasions would start building up in the girl again, and perhaps lead to a total breakdown. She saw my point.

Maria's account, as we first talked it over, largely confirmed what Leonides had told me. One thing she refused to say, though, and it was vital: she denied vigorously that Nikos had killed the people in the *Bodies* studio. She sat there beside her headmistress, looking hardly more than ten, yet with the light of obstinacy in her eyes. Nikos had loved her and she had loved him. He had killed himself because of the horrible things she had done. But he had not killed the people in the *Bodies* studio. She did not know who had, but she knew he had not.

"Let's go over it again," I said, wearied by her hard, repetitive denials, which were absolute in a final, childish way. "You got to know Vince Haggarty through the kids in the café?"

"Yes," she replied, looking straight at me and not at the headmistress. "And the man he worked with. A horrible man called Mick. And he kept using these kids in films, and paying them money . . . lots of money . . . And one day Vince and Mick were in the café, and Mick asked if there wasn't anything that I wanted terribly badly, and I said a new dress for the Christmas party. And he said perhaps it could be arranged."

"And when they offered you money to be in a film, you said yes?"

"Yes. And they said they'd introduce me to the nice man who'd be in the film with me."

"So you met him before the filming, did you?"

"Oh yes . . . Or I don't think I could have done it. We met one evening in the café, and then the others went off to film, and we walked down to Trafalgar Square, and sat there talking, and then we went to another café, and he bought me a wonderful fruit sundae there. He was so nice . . . I *thought* he was nice . . ."

"What did you talk about?"

"He told me about himself, and how he lived. He was a sportsman—a sort of weightlifter, I think—and how he gave his whole life to the sport. He told me about his father, who was in the army and was killed, and about this wonderful mother he has, who helps him enormously. And he told me about all the training he has to do in the gym, hour after hour . . ."

"Did he tell you his name?"

"He didn't want to. He said I was to call him 'Chuck,' but I thought that was silly, because he wasn't American. Anyway, when he went up to the counter to get me another Coke, I looked into his sports bag, and there was a label saying 'Denzil Crabtree,' and I called him 'Denny' after that, and he thought I must have heard Vince or Mick call him that, so he let me go on."

"Then soon afterwards you went to the studio and made the film?"

"Yes." The eyes dropped, and the hand went out to the headmistress's.

Had they told you what . . . what you'd have to do?"

"No," she spat out violently. "Of course they hadn't. I'd never have done it if they had. They said I just had to take my clothes off and . . . sort of play around for a bit. And I didn't like it, but I thought it was worth the money. But when I'd taken my clothes off, I went over to the bed, and we fooled around for a bit, and then suddenly . . ."

She broke off.

"That's all right," I said hurriedly. "I don't need to hear about that. Of course you were very upset after it happened?"

"Yes. I felt horrible. *Ill*, and . . . disgusting. And in the end I had to tell my mother."

"That was the Wednesday after, wasn't it? A week later?"

"That's right."

"That's the day your father takes off from the restaurant, isn't it?"

"Yes. He takes the evening off. He goes jogging in Green Park, and then he goes to a Greek club in Camden Town."

"Did he come in from the jogging while you and your mother were talking?"

"Yes. Just after I'd started telling her."

"And Nikos—when did he come in?"

"He didn't. He never did."

"Why did your father say he did, then?"

"I don't know, but he was . . . mistaken."

"When did Nikos hear about . . . all this?"

"One day . . . later . . . when they all came round. Nikos's family all come round to us once a fortnight, and we go there in the other week. I told him on the day they came round."

"I see. Getting back to your father. What exactly did he hear?"

"Everything. I told them both about Vince, and how he filmed there on Monday and Wednesday nights, and how he sometimes used the kids who hadn't got homes, who I'd met in the café. And I told them about the offer they made to me, and how I wanted that dress, and how he'd offered me sixty pounds. And I told them about Denny, and about how nice he'd been the first time, and all he'd told me . . . And then I told them about the filming . . . and what Denny did to me . . ."

"And your father went wild?"

She pondered how to reply.

"He was very angry."

"He went and got his gun, I suppose?"

"No. No, he didn't. He never went out at all. He and Mother put me to bed, and then they sat talking for a long time. I heard them."

The little, appealing, childish face had resumed that obstinate expression. I felt sure that she was lying. And yet the whole case didn't quite, somehow, make sense. Not psychological sense, as far as I understood the people involved. Leonides's story had certainly been a good one, a consistent one. I could see an adolescent boy, overhearing that story from his girlfriend, from the person who he'd come to think of as his future wife, going over the edge, going out, getting a weapon, and gunning down all and sundry in the *Bodies* studio. He wouldn't ask himself if they were all involved, or if he did he'd have said they were all in the same dirty game.

I couldn't quite see Leonides having the same rush of blood to the head, the same overmastering burst of unreason. Leonides—the impeccable restaurateur? The genial mine host of the Knossos? He might wait, stalk Vince Haggarty home, kill him—that I could imagine. But not to wait, just to rush out and kill all four? . . . And yet I must have misjudged him, because surely that's what must have happened . . . Unless there was something else, something *more* that drove him that one step further into blind passion.

In the back of my mind something clicked, a connection was made. Was it possible?

"You told your parents all Denny had told you about himself and his background, did you?"

"Yes."

"And did you tell them his name?"

She wriggled uncomfortably in her chair, not looking at me.

"I didn't want to."

"Why not?"

"Because . . . because I'd liked him . . . liked him at first . . . And then I didn't really blame him . . . He was more sort of . . . pathetic."

"But you did tell them?" She nodded. "Was that because your father demanded to know?"

"Yes."

"Demanded over and over again?"

"Yes . . . He shook me . . . In the end I had to tell him."

"And when you told him—Denzil Crabtree—what did he say?"

Tears were trickling down her cheeks, but she still prevaricated.

"I don't know. He talked Greek to my mother. I didn't understand. I don't know that much Greek."

I saw that I had to put it to her, and to have the courage of my hunch.

"I think you did understand, Maria. Because it wasn't anything very difficult, was it? Wasn't it something like: 'I killed his father, and now I'm going to kill him?'"

She broke down into sobs.

"Yes. That's what he shouted before he ran out. That's what he thought he was doing."

CHAPTER 19

I didn't really get to discuss the *Bodies* case in depth until about a week after I arrested Leonides. One bleak evening in early December Charlie arrived at the flat on a visit, sat in an armchair drinking cans of cold Australian beer, and demanded to be told all the details.

"I thought at first it was going to be difficult to get the necessary evidence," I told him. "I thought the Leonideses would be one of those families that close ranks impenetrably when they're threatened from outside. In fact, without ratting on her husband in any way, Elena has been surprisingly cooperative. When we took him, old Leonides wrung his hands and lamented the fate of his family, his restaurant, and so on. I think the idea of his indispensability was very important to him. In fact Elena has engaged a capable young chap to supervise the front of house, she remains in charge of the kitchen, and everything goes on swimmingly."

"And business is good, I suppose," said Charlie cynically.

"Business, disgustingly enough, is very brisk, and will remain so until after the trial, at the earliest."

"Elena was the cause of all the trouble with Denny's father, was she?"

"Oh yes. Back in Cyprus in 1965. It was only at the last minute that I remembered that Leonides was not in fact Greek, but Cypriot, and then I made the connection. How far the trouble went I haven't liked to inquire. After all, that's not a murder he's ever likely to be charged with. And with someone so likely to fly off the handle, the actual provocation could have been pretty small. It may be, though, that Elena has had something of a grudge against her husband ever since, and that's something that is helping us."

"Christ," mused Charlie, "to look at her now you wouldn't think she'd ever been something to kill over."

"She was probably one of those typical Mediterranean women who go from being a real prick-tickler to being a frump in no time at all."

"Like Sophia Loren, for example?" put in Jan sweetly.

"If there was any closing of the ranks," I went on, "it was between Leonides and his pal Stavros, Nikos's father. There was plenty there of the old male solidarity Jan goes on so boringly about. Did I tell you about the jogging shoes?"

"No."

"Well, it was the first thing we looked for, of course, but not surprisingly it was no go. Not a pair in the house. We thought we'd have to satisfy ourselves with that as evidence: the fact that a regular jogger apparently owned not a single pair of jogging shoes. But do you know what he'd done with them?"

Charlie thought.

"Given them to his pal Stavros to put among Nikos's things?"

"Right! Isn't it incredible? That Stavros should do it? He swore blind they were his son's, and has never gone back on that. Of course Forensic reduced that little claim to mincemeat, and that will be an important part of the evidence against him. You can't get away with clever-cleverness like that these days. But it's very interesting on the human level, isn't it?"

"What other evidence have you?" asked Charlie, getting up to get himself his third can of beer, which, to be fair, he had brought along himself, ready chilled.

"No gun, of course. Got rid of immediately. My bet is that it was put in one of those garbage bins in Soho. Easiest way. But the best evidence against him will come from Haggarty and Spivey, because they actually saw him."

"Saw him. How?"

"Because, as I half suspected, if Bob Cordle's session went on too long because of Wayne Flushing's incompetence as a model, then the unlovely Vince and Mick would be around in the area waiting for the lights to go off, and for Bob and his models to come out of the building and go home. Then they'd hop straight in and set the cameras rolling. They didn't let the grass grow under their feet, those two, as the catalogue of films proved. They'd botched together a fantastic *number* of films, leaving questions of quality aside. And of course, where would they be waiting but in the café opposite? From there, instead of seeing Cordle and Co. come out, they saw Leonides run in, disappear up the stairs, and run out again after six shots had been fired."

"Did they connect the two things?"

"Not at first. They thought it was the Strip à la Wild West, naturally. But then nobody came out of *Bodies,* and they waited and waited, and still nobody came out, and finally Vince went in, heard nothing, went upstairs, saw the bodies, and then ran for his life."

"Did he realize who it was who'd done it?"

"Yes. He knew Leonides. Vince is an old Soho hand."

"Did he realize he was one of the intended victims?"

"He didn't *know*—he could never be sure. But he had a bloody good idea. He didn't come within a mile of Windlesham Street from then on. They had to keep quiet about it, of course, because if they let on to us they'd spoil their own game. And apart from that they were dead scared. Someone who'd just wiped out four people wasn't going to balk at a fifth and a sixth. For a time they were very frightened people."

"Will they make good witnesses, though?" asked Jan.

"No. We're a little bit worried about that. We'll use Haggarty rather than Spivey, but even so he's not a type any jury is going to love and trust. Still, he's the best we've got, and in fact everything he says will be gospel truth. I don't think there's any doubt we'll get a conviction."

"I'm sorry for the little girl," said Jan. "First that

awful experience, then the boyfriend killing himself, then Father taken from her as well."

"Yes," I said. "Under all that, she's bearing up remarkably well. It's good that we probably won't need to use her in the trial. I think in fact the losing of Father may prove a blessing in disguise: Leonides was a patriarch without the real patriarchal equipment—more bluster than authority. I think the process of growing up may be easier without him. I'm afraid poor Nikos would never have come to much. By all accounts he was a neurotic boy, smothered by his father who was still fighting the Greek Civil War, and full of mad macho notions the boy could never have lived up to. Maybe that's why he took the news the way he did. I'm as sorry for that boy as for anyone. Poor Maria, poor Nikos—poor Denny, even. It was a sad, sorry case, but I think Maria and her mother are going to come out of it all right."

"There's something else I wanted to talk to you about," said Charlie, draining his can.

"I know."

"You can't. It's something different. I've never mentioned it."

"You want to talk about joining the police force."

"Damn it, how did you—?"

"Oh, come on, Charlie. You've been smart-arsing it throughout this case. Give me credit for some native powers of observation just this once. It's been obvious to me for weeks."

"Well," said Charlie, rather miffed, "tell me what you think."

I had anticipated it, and had thought about it.

"We'll skip the bit where I tell you that policing isn't

all fun and raids and arrests, and dressing up and pretending, like it's been for you these last few weeks—right?"

"Right. Mostly *un*dressing and pretending, actually."

"We can't skip the bit where I tell you it's nearly all slog, ninety percent of it, sheer bloody tedium. And when it isn't, it's less likely to be exciting than just plain nasty. Stomach-turning, very often. And don't tell me you've got a strong stomach, because you just can't know. You've only seen one stiff in your life, and that was a nice clean one."

"Point taken. But I think I could cope."

"Have you thought about all the racist talk you'll have to put up with?"

"So—where's the difference from now?"

"Not just from the public—from colleagues: the chap with you on the beat, the blokes you drink with in the canteen."

"Where's the difference?"

"People expect the police to be different."

"I don't. You're not bleeding clergymen. It's just a job. It's pretty much the same inside the Force as outside, I reckon."

"That's a point of view," I admitted. "We don't get the police we deserve, we get the police we *are.* Have you got the necessary educational qualifications?"

Charlie shot me the sort of look that reminded me that he'd struck me as a distinctly formidable character when I'd seen him first.

"Do you *mind?* I thought *everyone* had the educational qualifications you demand for the police," he said nastily.

"Well—if it were up to me, I'd say Welcome to the Police," I said.

"Oh—I haven't made up my mind," said Charlie, going all hard-to-get. "There's other possibilities. I may have got the bug for the posing game. Who knows what offers I may get when the next issue of *Fly* comes out?"

"That magazine will be a grave embarrassment to you, once you're in the Force," I said, ignoring his coyness.

"Crap. I won't be the first policeman to have done embarrassing things in the line of duty. At least I didn't have to go into drag."

"Tell me," said Jan. "When you were involved in the case, who did you *guess* had done it? Obviously you wouldn't guess Mr. Leonides, because there was nothing to connect him with it till right at the end. Who did you *guess?*"

"Policemen don't *guess* like that," I said. "Except in their sleepless-night reveries."

"Bullshit," said Jan. "Anyway, who did you pick on in your reveries?"

"Todd Masterman," I said. "Though it did occur to me once that Denny Crabtree's mum had the guts to do it. And was just slightly bonkers on one subject, but perfectly compos otherwise."

"Who did *you* guess?" Jan asked Charlie.

"Mick Spivey. But that was pure emotion, pure distaste for the guy. I knew he hadn't got the guts to do anything like that. I suppose if I'd thought about it, I'd have plumped for Masterman as well."

"Funny—I'd have plumped for Phil Fennilow," said Jan. "He sounded so yucky-looking, and then he obviously fitted well into his grubby occupation—and it *is* grubby, whatever you may say. He was at the very centre of the business, yet you never seem to have considered him, Perry."

"I suppose—as with Leonides—it was because I'd known him before. It's funny—silly—but if you've known them in some other connection, you never think they're going to pop up as murderers."

"Oh, of course, you met him when you were on that Vice Squad job, didn't you? Actually talked to him."

"Yes. We talked in a pub."

"He doesn't sound like the sort of person you'd normally talk to in a pub. What did you talk *about?*"

I looked daggers at Jan. What a wonderful instinct she has for the tender spot.

"Well, if you must know," I said with dignity, "we were both in this pub and he approached me . . ."

"Yes?"

"Actually he asked me if I'd care to be photographed for *Bodies* magazine."

Charlie let out a yelp of laughter, then threw himself hugely around in his chair, squirming with delight, and throwing back his head in a series of delighted chortles.

"Man!" he said, wiping his eyes. "That must have been some time ago!"

I could have killed him. Next day I got back into a serious training programme at the Scotland Yard gym.

ABOUT THE AUTHOR

Robert Barnard has been nominated four times for mystery writing's highest honor, the Edgar Award. His most recent books include *Corpse in a Gilded Cage, Out of the Blackout, Fête Fatale,* and *Political Suicide.* For seven years he was Professor of English Literature at the University of Tromsø in Norway, the northernmost university in the world. He and his wife, Louise, now live in Leeds, England.